PENGUIN POPULAR CLASSICS

MUCH ADO ABOUT NOTHING

BY WILLIAM SHAKESPEARE

PENGUIN POPULAR CLASSICS

MUCH ADO ABOUT NOTHING

WILLIAM SHAKESPEARE

PENGUIN BOOKS

PENGUIN BOOKS

Published by the Penguin Group
Penguin Books Ltd, 80 Strand, London WC2R 0RL, England
Penguin Putnam Inc., 375 Hudson Street, New York, New York 10014, USA
Penguin Books Australia Ltd, Ringwood, Victoria, Australia
Penguin Books Canada Ltd, 10 Alcorn Avenue, Toronto, Ontario, Canada M4V 3B2
Penguin Books India (P) Ltd, 11 Community Centre, Panchsheel Park,
New Delhi – 110 017, India
Penguin Books (NZ) Ltd, Cnr Rosedale and Airborne Roads, Albany, Auckland,
New Zealand
Penguin Books (South Africa) (Pty), 24 Sturdee Avenue, Rosebank 2196, South Africa

Penguin Books Ltd, Registered Offices: 80 Strand, London WC2R 0RL, England

www.penguin.com

First published 1598
Published in Penguin Popular Classics 1997
11

Printed in England by Cox & Wyman Ltd, Reading, Berkshire

CONTENTS

THE WORKS OF SHAKESPEARE

PLAYS

APPROXIMATE DATE		FIRST PRINTED
Before 1594	HENRY VI *three parts*	*Folio* 1623
	RICHARD III	1597
	TITUS ANDRONICUS	1594
	LOVE'S LABOUR'S LOST	1598
	THE TWO GENTLEMEN OF VERONA	*Folio*
	THE COMEDY OF ERRORS	*Folio*
	THE TAMING OF THE SHREW	*Folio*
1594–1597	ROMEO AND JULIET (*pirated* 1597)	1599
	A MIDSUMMER NIGHT'S DREAM	1600
	RICHARD II	1597
	KING JOHN	*Folio*
	THE MERCHANT OF VENICE	1600
1597–1600	HENRY IV *part i*	1598
	HENRY IV *part ii*	1600
	HENRY V (*pirated* 1600)	*Folio*
	MUCH ADO ABOUT NOTHING	1600
	MERRY WIVES OF WINDSOR (*pirated* 1602)	*Folio*
	AS YOU LIKE IT	*Folio*
	JULIUS CAESAR	*Folio*
	TROYLUS AND CRESSIDA	1609
1601–1608	HAMLET (*pirated* 1603)	1604
	TWELFTH NIGHT	*Folio*
	MEASURE FOR MEASURE	*Folio*
	ALL'S WELL THAT ENDS WELL	*Folio*
	OTHELLO	1622
	LEAR	1608
	MACBETH	*Folio*
	TIMON OF ATHENS	*Folio*
	ANTONY AND CLEOPATRA	*Folio*
	CORIOLANUS	*Folio*
After 1608	PERICLES (*omitted from the Folio*)	1609
	CYMBELINE	*Folio*
	THE WINTER'S TALE	*Folio*
	THE TEMPEST	*Folio*
	HENRY VIII	*Folio*

POEMS

DATES UNKNOWN		
	VENUS AND ADONIS	1593
	THE RAPE OF LUCRECE	1594
	SONNETS	1609
	A LOVER'S COMPLAINT	
	THE PHOENIX AND THE TURTLE	1601

WILLIAM SHAKESPEARE

William Shakespeare was born at Stratford upon Avon in April, 1564. He was the third child, and eldest son, of John Shakespeare and Mary Arden. His father was one of the most prosperous men of Stratford, who held in turn the chief offices in the town. His mother was of gentle birth, the daughter of Robert Arden of Wilmcote. In December, 1582, Shakespeare married Ann Hathaway, daughter of a farmer of Shottery, near Stratford; their first child Susanna was baptized on May 6, 1583, and twins, Hamnet and Judith, on February 22, 1585. Little is known of Shakespeare's early life; but it is unlikely that a writer who dramatized such an incomparable range and variety of human kinds and experiences should have spent his early manhood entirely in placid pursuits in a country town. There is one tradition, not universally accepted, that he fled from Stratford because he was in trouble for deer stealing, and had fallen foul of Sir Thomas Lucy, the local magnate; another that he was for some time a schoolmaster.

From 1592 onwards the records are much fuller. In March, 1592, the Lord Strange's players produced a new play at the Rose Theatre called *Harry the Sixth*, which was very successful, and was probably the *First Part of Henry VI*. In the autumn of 1592 Robert Greene, the best known of the professional writers, as he was dying wrote a letter to three fellow writers in which he warned them against the ingratitude of players in general, and in particular against an 'upstart crow' who 'supposes he is as much able to bombast out a blank verse as the best of you: and being an absolute Johannes Factotum is in his own conceit the only

Shake-scene in a country'. This is the first reference to Shakespeare, and the whole passage suggests that Shakespeare had become suddenly famous as a playwright. At this time Shakespeare was brought into touch with Edward Alleyne the great tragedian, and Christopher Marlowe, whose thundering parts of Tamburlaine, the Jew of Malta, and Dr Faustus Alleyne was acting, as well as Hieronimo, the hero of Kyd's *Spanish Tragedy*, the most famous of all Elizabethan plays.

In April, 1593, Shakespeare published his poem *Venus and Adonis*, which was dedicated to the young Earl of Southampton: it was a great and lasting success, and was reprinted nine times in the next few years. In May, 1594, his second poem, *The Rape of Lucrece*, was also dedicated to Southampton.

There was little playing in 1593, for the theatres were shut during a severe outbreak of the plague; but in the autumn of 1594, when the plague ceased, the playing companies were reorganized, and Shakespeare became a sharer in the Lord Chamberlain's company who went to play in the Theatre in Shoreditch. During these months Marlowe and Kyd had died. Shakespeare was thus for a time without a rival. He had already written the three parts of *Henry VI*, *Richard III*, *Titus Andronicus*, *The Two Gentlemen of Verona*, *Love's Labour's Lost*, *The Comedy of Errors*, and *The Taming of the Shrew*. Soon afterwards he wrote the first of his greater plays – *Romeo and Juliet* – and he followed this success in the next three years with *A Midsummer Night's Dream*, *Richard II*, and *The Merchant of Venice*. The two parts of *Henry IV*, introducing Falstaff, the most popular of all his comic characters, were written in 1597-8.

The company left the Theatre in 1597 owing to disputes over a renewal of the ground lease, and went to play at the

Curtain in the same neighbourhood. The disputes continued throughout 1598, and at Christmas the players settled the matter by demolishing the old Theatre and re-erecting a new playhouse on the South bank of the Thames, near Southwark Cathedral. This playhouse was named the Globe. The expenses of the new building were shared by the chief members of the Company, including Shakespeare, who was now a man of some means. In 1596 he had bought New Place, a large house in the centre of Stratford, for £60, and through his father purchased a coat-of-arms from the Heralds, which was the official recognition that he and his family were gentlefolk.

By the summer of 1598 Shakespeare was recognized as the greatest of English dramatists. Booksellers were printing his more popular plays, at times even in pirated or stolen versions, and he received a remarkable tribute from a young writer named Francis Meres, in his book *Palladis Tamia*. In a long catalogue of English authors Meres gave Shakespeare more prominence than any other writer, and mentioned by name twelve of his plays.

Shortly before the Globe was opened, Shakespeare had completed the cycle of plays dealing with the whole story of the Wars of the Roses with *Henry V*. It was followed by *As You Like it*, and *Julius Caesar*, the first of the maturer tragedies. In the next three years he wrote *Troilus and Cressida*, *The Merry Wives of Windsor*, *Hamlet*, and *Twelfth Night*.

On March 24, 1603, Queen Elizabeth died. The company had often performed before her, but they found her successor a far more enthusiastic patron. One of the first acts of King James was to take over the company and to promote them to be his own servants so that henceforward they were known as the King's Men. They acted now very frequently at Court, and prospered accordingly. In the early years of the reign Shakespeare wrote the more sombre comedies, *All's Well that Ends Well*, and *Measure for Measure*, which were followed by *Othello*, *Macbeth*, and *King Lear*. Then he returned to Roman themes with *Antony and Cleopatra*, and *Coriolanus*.

Since 1601 Shakespeare had been writing less, and there were now a number of rival dramatists who were introducing new styles of drama, particularly Ben Jonson (whose first successful comedy, *Every Man in his Humour*, was acted by Shakespeare's company in 1598), Chapman, Dekker, Marston, and Beaumont and Fletcher who began to write in 1607. In 1608 the King's Men acquired a second playhouse, an indoor private theatre in the fashionable quarter of the Blackfriars. At private theatres, plays were performed indoors; the prices charged were higher than in the public playhouses, and the audience consequently was more select. Shakespeare seems to have retired from the stage about this time: his name does not occur in the various lists of players after 1607. Henceforward he lived for the most part at Stratford, where he was regarded as one of the most important citizens. He still wrote a few plays, and he tried his hand at the new form of tragi-comedy – a play with tragic incidents but a happy ending – which Beaumont and Fletcher had popularized. He wrote four of these – *Pericles*, *Cymbeline*, *The Winter's Tale*, and *The Tempest*, which was acted at Court in 1611. For the last four years of his life he lived in retirement. His son Hamnet had died in 1596: his two daughters were now married. Shakespeare died at Stratford upon Avon on April 23, 1616, and was buried in the chancel of the church, before the high altar. Shortly afterwards a memorial which still exists, with a portrait bust, was set up on the North wall. His wife survived him.

When Shakespeare died fourteen of his plays had been separately published in Quarto booklets. In 1623 his surviving fellow actors, John Heming and Henry Condell, with the co-operation of a number of printers, published a collected edition of thirty-six plays in one Folio volume, with an engraved portrait, memorial verses by Ben Jonson and others, and an Epistle to the Reader in which Heming and Condell make the interesting note that Shakespeare's 'hand and mind went together, and what he thought, he uttered with that easiness that we have scarce received from him a blot in his papers'.

The plays as printed in the Quartos or the Folio differ considerably from the usual modern text. They are often not divided into scenes, and sometimes not even into acts. Nor are there place-headings at the beginning of each scene, because in the Elizabethan theatre there was no scenery. They are carelessly printed and the spelling is erratic.

THE ELIZABETHAN THEATRE

Although plays of one sort and another had been acted for many generations, no permanent playhouse was erected in England until 1576. In the 1570's the Lord Mayor and Aldermen of the City of London and the players were constantly at variance. As a result James Burbage, then the leader of the great Earl of Leicester's players, decided that he would erect a playhouse outside the jurisdiction of the Lord Mayor, where the players would no longer be hindered by the authorities. Accordingly in 1576 he built the Theatre in Shoreditch, at that time a suburb of London. The experiment was successful, and by 1592 there were two more playhouses in London, the Curtain (also in Shoreditch), and the Rose on the south bank of the river, near Southwark Cathedral.

Elizabethan players were accustomed to act on a variety of stages; in the great hall of a nobleman's house, or one of the Queen's palaces, in town halls and in yards, as well as their own theatre.

The public playhouse for which most of Shakespeare's plays were written was a small and intimate affair. The outside measurement of the Fortune Theatre, which was built in 1600 to rival the new Globe, was but eighty feet square. Playhouses were usually circular or octagonal, with three tiers of galleries looking down upon the yard or pit, which was open to the sky. The stage jutted out into the yard so that the actors came forward into the midst of their audience.

Over the stage there was a roof, and on either side doors by which the characters entered or disappeared. Over the back of the stage ran a gallery or upper stage which was used whenever an upper scene was needed, as when Romeo climbs up to Juliet's bedroom, or the citizens of Angiers address King John from the walls. The space beneath this upper stage was known as the tiring house; it was concealed from the audience by a curtain which would be drawn back to reveal an inner stage, for such scenes as the witches' cave in *Macbeth*, Prospero's cell, or Juliet's tomb.

There was no general curtain concealing the whole stage, so that all scenes on the main stage began with an entrance and ended with an exit. Thus in tragedies the dead must be carried away. There was no scenery, and therefore no limit to the number of scenes, for a scene came to an end when the characters left the stage. When it was necessary for the exact locality of a scene to be known, then Shakespeare

THE GLOBE THEATRE

Wood-engraving by R. J. Beedham after a reconstruction by J. C. Adams

indicated it in the dialogue; otherwise a simple property or a garment was sufficient; a chair or stool showed an indoor scene, a man wearing riding boots was a messenger, a king wearing armour was on the battlefield, or the like. Such simplicity was on the whole an advantage; the spectator was not distracted by the setting and Shakespeare was able to use as many scenes as he wished. The action passed by very quickly: a play of 2500 lines of verse could be acted in two hours. Moreover, since the actor was so close to his audience, the slightest subtlety of voice and gesture was easily appreciated.

The company was a 'Fellowship of Players', who were all partners and sharers. There were usually ten to fifteen full members, with three or four boys, and some paid servants. Shakespeare had therefore to write for his team. The chief actor in the company was Richard Burbage, who first distinguished himself as Richard III; for him Shakespeare wrote his great tragic parts. An important member of the company was the clown or low comedian. From 1594 to 1600 the company's clown was Will Kemp; he was succeeded by Robert Armin. No women were allowed to appear on the stage, and all women's parts were taken by boys.

MUCH ADO ABOUT NOTHING

Much Ado About Nothing was written before the summer of 1600, and probably in 1598. In the Stationers' Register there is a casual note dated 4th August [1600] that four plays of the Lord Chamberlain's Company are 'to be staied', i.e., not printed. These plays were *As You Like it, Henry the Fifth,* Ben Jonson's *Every Man in his Humour,* and *Much Ado About Nothing.* On the 23rd August the play was regularly entered for printing, together with the *Second Part of Henry the Fourth,* as the property of the printers Andrew Wise and William Aspley. Wise had already printed Shakespeare's *Richard the Second, Richard the Third, The First Part of Henry the Fourth.* Soon afterwards a quarto was published with the title-page:

Much adoe about Nothing. As it hath been sundrie times publikely acted by the right honourable, the Lord Chamberlaine his seruants. Written by William Shakespeare. London. Printed by V. S. for Andrew Wise, and William Aspley. 1600.

As is usual in Shakespeare's comedies, the plot is made up of several incidents. The main story tells how Claudio, having fallen in love with Hero, is persuaded to believe that he has seen Borachio converse with her at her bedroom window on the night before the wedding, and is thus led to repudiate her. Such a motive, in various forms, was fairly common in tales of the sixteenth century: one version is told by Spenser in *The Faerie Queene,* Book II, Canto iv. The nearest to the play is one of the Italian novels of Matteo Bandello, of which the plot is as follows:

In the year 1283 after the massacre of the French in Sicily by the Sicilians, known as the Sicilian Vespers, King Pedro of Arragon seized the island. While his court was being held at Messina, one of his knights called Don Timbreo di Cardona fell in love with a young lady named Fenicia, daughter of Lionato de Lionati, and she with him. He sent a friend to ask for the lady's hand and to everyone's satisfaction the marriage day was appointed. But another knight, Signor Girondo Olerio Valentiano, had also fallen in love with Fenicia, and pondered how he could cause discord between Timbreo and Fenicia and thereby win the lady for himself. He therefore persuaded a young man to tell Don Timbreo that Fenicia had a lover, who visited her secretly: furthermore he would so place Don Timbreo that he might watch the lovers meeting. Accordingly Don Timbreo hid himself in the garden of Lionato. After a time he saw the young gentleman pass by with two companions carrying a ladder, and he heard one of them warning the others to be careful with the ladder for the last time the Lady Fenicia had complained that they made too much noise. The ladder was placed against the wall, and one of the men climbed up and entered a window.

Next morning Don Timbreo sent a messenger to Lionato whom he found with Fenicia, her mother, and her two sisters. The messenger having first obtained a promise that he should not be injured if his mission was unwelcome then delivered his message. Don Timbreo, he said, had with his own eyes perceived that Fenicia was disloyal to him, and therefore bade her provide herself with another husband. Fenicia was so shocked by this unexpected accusation that she fell down in a swoon. She was put to bed and partly restored to life, but soon afterwards she fell again into so deep a swoon that the physicians declared her to be dead. When all had departed, her mother and her aunt began to wash the body for burial. Fenicia opened her eyes, and the women saw that she was alive. So Lionato was summoned and they agreed that the funeral should proceed, and that meanwhile Fenicia should be secretly sent away into the country.

The report of Fenicia's death caused great sorrow in Messina, for when the case was examined the evidence on which Don Timbreo had condemned her appeared very slight and improbable. Don Timbreo was thus filled with remorse; as also was Signor Girondo, insomuch that he confessed his treacherous trick to Don Timbreo. Don Timbreo forgave him but made him promise to help in the restoring of Fenicia's good name. They therefore went to Lionato, and Timbreo declared that he would recompense the injured father by obeying any command that should be laid on him. Lionato replied that since Don Timbreo had a desire to marry he must take the lady whom he would offer. To this Timbreo agreed.

A year had now passed. Fenicia was living under the name of Lucilla. Her health was so greatly improved in the country that she was hardly recognizable. In fulfilment of the agreement Lionato arranged that Don Timbreo, accompanied by Signor Girondo and his friends, should hear Mass at a village outside Messina and should there meet the lady whose name was Lucilla (which was the name borne by Fenicia in her hiding). The Mass over, Lucilla was brought out and the marriage was performed. Then followed the feast, when all was revealed and the lovers were happily reconciled. Girondo humbly begged Fenicia's pardon, and the day's rejoicings were completed by Girondo's betrothal to Belfiore, Fenicia's sister.

There is some connexion between story and play in the coincidence of the names Don Pedro, Lionato, and Messina, but the details vary so considerably that it is not likely that

Shakespeare used Bandello's story at first hand. More probably he based *Much Ado About Nothing* on some other play.

There are maybe traces of this old play in the original Quarto text of *Much Ado*. The opening stage direction reads *Enter Leonato, Governor of Messina, Innogen his wife, Hero his daughter, and Beatrice his niece, with a messenger*. The wife reappears in the Quarto in the stage direction at the opening of Act II, Scene 1, but she has no part whatever in the play and is always omitted by editors and producers. Moreover the devices by which Borachio caused Margaret to impersonate Hero and Hero to sleep in some other bedroom are not satisfactorily explained in the play in its present form. The arguments (some of which are recorded in the Notes) for supposing that *Much Ado* was thus a revised play are elaborately worked out in his edition in *The New Shakespeare* by Dr Dover Wilson, who also argues that the Quarto text was set up directly from the playhouse copy in Shakespeare's own handwriting.

The Quarto is fairly well printed, and there are few real difficulties in the text itself. There are no divisions into Acts and Scenes. Several essential *exits* and *entries* are omitted, and the speakers' names are often confused. Thus Antonio, Leonato's brother, appears usually as *Old* [*Old Man*] or *Brother*; Don Pedro is *Pedro* and *Prince*. The most interesting confusion is in the names of Dogberry and Verges who in Act IV, Scene 2 become 'Kemp' and 'Cowley', these being the names of the actors who took their parts. Such inconsistencies are natural enough in the original manuscript of an author who was writing a play for a particular company.

The play was not reprinted until it appeared in the First Folio in 1623, when the Folio text was set up from a copy of the Quarto which had been slightly revised. A number of small errors were corrected, and a number of new errors added. Act divisions but not scene divisions omitted in the Quarto were added in the Folio.

The present text follows the Quarto closely in its arrangement and readings, and particularly in the punctuation, except where the original seemed obviously wrong. The modern custom is to punctuate according to syntax; Elizabethan punctuation was intended as a guide for recitation or reading aloud. The punctuation in the Quarto is light, and, especially in the prose speeches, confined chiefly to commas and colons; but on the whole it is very effective and shows how the players spoke their lines, for *Much Ado* is essentially a play of quick speech, with few of the pauses and silences so effective in Shakespeare's tragedies. These touches have been obliterated in the normalized punctuation of the 'accepted text'. The present text keeps closely to the Quarto and may therefore in some ways seem unusual to those familiar with the 'accepted text' but it is nearer to the play as performed by Shakespeare's own company.

THE ACTORS' NAMES

DON PEDRO, prince of Arragon
DON JOHN, his bastard brother
CLAUDIO, a young lord of Florence
BENEDICK, a young lord of Padua
LEONATO, governor of Messina
ANTONIO, his brother
BALTHASAR, attendant on Don Pedro
CONRADE } followers of Don John
BORACHIO
FRIAR FRANCIS
DOGBERRY, a constable
VERGES, a headborough
A SEXTON
A BOY
HERO, daughter to Leonato
BEATRICE, niece to Leonato
MARGARET } gentlewomen attending on Hero
URSULA

Messengers, Watch, Attendants, etc.

Much Ado About Nothing

I.1

Enter Leonato, Governor of Messina, Innogen his wife,
Hero his daughter, and Beatrice his niece, with a messenger.

LEONATO: I learn in this letter, that Don Pedro of Arragon
comes this night to Messina. 5

MESSENGER: He is very near by this, he was not three
leagues off when I left him.

LEONATO: How many gentlemen have you lost in this
action?

MESSENGER: But few of any sort, and none of name. 10

LEONATO: A victory is twice itself, when the achiever
brings home full numbers: I find here, that Don Pedro
hath bestowed much honour on a young Florentine called Claudio.

MESSENGER: Much deserv'd on his part, and equally re- 15
member'd by Don Pedro, he hath borne himself beyond
the promise of his age, doing in the figure of a lamb, the
feats of a lion, he hath indeed better better'd expectation
than you must expect of me to tell you how.

LEONATO: He hath an uncle here in Messina will be very 20
much glad of it.

MESSENGER: I have already delivered him letters, and there
appears much joy in him, even so much, that joy could
not show itself modest enough, without a badge of bitterness. 25

LEONATO: Did he break out into tears?

MESSENGER: In great measure.

LEONATO: A kind overflow of kindness, there are no faces
truer than those that are so wash'd. How much better is
it to weep at joy, than to joy at weeping! 30

BEATRICE: I pray you, is Signior Mountanto return'd from the wars or no?

MESSENGER: I know none of that name, Lady, there was none such in the army of any sort.

5　LEONATO: What is he that you ask for niece?

HERO: My cousin means Signior Benedick of Padua.

MESSENGER: O he 's return'd, and as pleasant as ever he was.

BEATRICE: He set up his bills here in Messina, and chal-
10　leng'd Cupid at the flight, and my uncle's fool reading the challenge subscrib'd for Cupid, and challeng'd him at the burbolt: I pray you, how many hath he kill'd and eaten in these wars? But how many hath he kill'd? for indeed I promised to eat all of his killing.

15　LEONATO: Faith niece you tax Signior Benedick too much, but he 'll be meet with you, I doubt it not.

MESSENGER: He hath done good service Lady in these wars.

BEATRICE: You had musty victual, and he hath holp to eat
20　it, he is a very valiant trencher man, he hath an excellent stomach.

MESSENGER: And a good soldier too, Lady.

BEATRICE: And a good soldier to a Lady, but what is he to a Lord?

25　MESSENGER: A Lord to a Lord, a man to a man, stuff'd with all honourable virtues.

BEATRICE: It is so indeed, he is no less than a stuff'd man, but for the stuffing well, we are all mortal.

LEONATO: You must not, sir, mistake my niece. There is a
30　kind of merry war betwixt Signior Benedick and her, they never meet but there 's a skirmish of wit between them.

BEATRICE: Alas he gets nothing by that, in our last con-

flict, four of his five wits went halting off, and now is the
whole man govern'd with one, so that if he have wit
enough to keep himself warm, let him bear it for a differ-
ence between himself and his horse, for it is all the wealth
that he hath left, to be known a reasonable creature. Who 5
is his companion now? he hath every month a new sworn
brother.

MESSENGER: Is 't possible?

BEATRICE: Very easily possible, he wears his faith but
as the fashion of his hat, it ever changes with the next 10
block.

MESSENGER: I see Lady the gentleman is not in your books.

BEATRICE: No, and he were, I would burn my study, but
I pray you who is his companion? Is there no young
squarer now that will make a voyage with him to the 15
devil?

MESSENGER: He is most in the company of the right noble
Claudio.

BEATRICE: O Lord, he will hang upon him like a disease,
he is sooner caught than the pestilence, and the taker runs 20
presently mad, God help the noble Claudio, if he have
caught the Benedick, it will cost him a thousand pound
ere a' be cured.

MESSENGER: I will hold friends with you Lady.

BEATRICE: Do good friend. 25

LEONATO: You will never run mad niece.

BEATRICE: No, not till a hot January.

MESSENGER: Don Pedro is approach'd.

   Enter Don Pedro, Claudio, Benedick, Balthasar, and
               John the Bastard. 30

DON PEDRO: Good Signior Leonato, are you come to
meet your trouble: the fashion of the world is, to avoid
cost, and you encounter it.

LEONATO: Never came trouble to my house, in the like-
ness of your Grace, for trouble being gone, comfort
should remain: but when you depart from me, sorrow
abides, and happiness takes his leave.

5 DON PEDRO: You embrace your charge too willingly: I
think this is your daughter.

LEONATO: Her mother hath many times told me so.

BENEDICK: Were you in doubt sir that you ask'd her?

LEONATO: Signior Benedick, no, for then were you a child.

10 DON PEDRO: You have it full Benedick, we may guess by
this, what you are, being a man. Truly the Lady fathers
herself: be happy Lady, for you are like an honourable
father.

BENEDICK: If Signior Leonato be her father, she would not
15 have his head on her shoulders for all Messina as like him
as she is.

BEATRICE: I wonder that you will still be talking, Signior
Benedick, nobody marks you.

BENEDICK: What my dear Lady Disdain! are you yet liv-
20 ing?

BEATRICE: Is it possible Disdain should die, while she hath
such meet food to feed it, as Signior Benedick? Courtesy
itself must convert to Disdain, if you come in her presence.

25 BENEDICK: Then is courtesy a turn-coat, but it is certain I
am loved of all Ladies, only you excepted: and I would
I could find in my heart that I had not a hard heart, for
truly I love none.

BEATRICE: A dear happiness to women, they would else
30 have been troubled with a pernicious suitor: I thank God
and my cold blood, I am of your humour for that, I had
rather hear my dog bark at a crow, than a man swear he
loves me.

BENEDICK: God keep your Ladyship still in that mind, so some gentleman or other shall 'scape a predestinate scratch'd face.

BEATRICE: Scratching could not make it worse, and 'twere such a face as yours were.   5

BENEDICK: Well, you are a rare parrot teacher.

BEATRICE: A bird of my tongue, is better than a beast of yours.

BENEDICK: I would my horse had the speed of your tongue, and so good a continuer, but keep your way a' 10 God's name, I have done.

BEATRICE: You always end with a jade's trick, I know you of old.

DON PEDRO: That is the sum of all: Leonato, Signior Claudio, and Signior Benedick, my dear friend Leonato, 15 hath invited you all: I tell him we shall stay here, at the least a month, and he heartily prays some occasion may detain us longer: I dare swear he is no hypocrite, but prays from his heart.

LEONATO: If you swear, my Lord, you shall not be for- 20 sworn: let me bid you welcome, my Lord, being recon- ciled to the Prince your brother: I owe you all duty.

JOHN: I thank you, I am not of many words, but I thank you.

LEONATO: Please it your Grace lead on?   25

DON PEDRO: Your hand Leonato, we will go together.

Exeunt. Manent Benedick and Claudio.

CLAUDIO: Benedick, didst thou note the daughter of Sig- nior Leonato?

BENEDICK: I noted her not, but I look'd on her.   30

CLAUDIO: Is she not a modest young lady?

BENEDICK: Do you question me as an honest man should do, for my simple true judgement? or would you have

me speak after my custom, as being a professed tyrant to
their sex?

CLAUDIO: No, I pray thee speak in sober judgement.

BENEDICK: Why i' faith methinks she's too low for a high
5   praise, too brown for a fair praise, and too little for a
great praise, only this commendation I can afford her,
that were she other than she is, she were unhandsome,
and being no other, but as she is, I do not like her.

CLAUDIO: Thou thinkest I am in sport, I pray thee tell me
10   truly how thou lik'st her.

BENEDICK: Would you buy her that you inquire after her?

CLAUDIO: Can the world buy such a jewel?

BENEDICK: Yea, and a case to put it into, but speak you
this with a sad brow? or do you play the flouting Jack, to
15   tell us Cupid is a good hare-finder, and Vulcan a rare
carpenter: Come, in what key shall a man take you to go
in the song?

CLAUDIO: In mine eye, she is the sweetest Lady that ever I
look'd on.

20 BENEDICK: I can see yet without spectacles, and I see no
such matter: there's her cousin, and she were not possess'd with a fury, exceeds her as much in beauty, as the
first of May doth the last of December: but I hope you
have no intent to turn husband, have you?

25 CLAUDIO: I would scarce trust myself, though I had sworn
the contrary, if Hero would be my wife.

BENEDICK: Is't come to this? In faith hath not the world
one man but he will wear his cap with suspicion? shall I
never see a bachelor of threescore again? go to i' faith,
30   and thou wilt needs thrust thy neck into a yoke, wear the
print of it, and sigh away Sundays: look, Don Pedro is
returned to seek you.

              Enter Don Pedro.

DON PEDRO: What secret hath held you here, that you followed not to Leonato's?

BENEDICK: I would your Grace would constrain me to tell.

DON PEDRO: I charge thee on thy allegiance.

BENEDICK: You hear, Count Claudio, I can be secret as a 5
dumb man, I would have you think so (but on my allegiance, mark you this, on my allegiance) he is in love, with who? now that is your Grace's part: mark how short his answer is, with Hero Leonato's short daughter.

CLAUDIO: If this were so, so were it utter'd.   10

BENEDICK: Like the old tale, my Lord, it is not so, nor 'twas not so: but indeed, God forbid it should be so.

CLAUDIO: If my passion change not shortly, God forbid it should be otherwise.

DON PEDRO: Amen, if you love her, for the Lady is very 15
well worthy.

CLAUDIO: You speak this to fetch me in, my Lord.

DON PEDRO: By my troth I speak my thought.

CLAUDIO: And in faith, my Lord, I spoke mine.

BENEDICK: And by my two faiths and troths, my Lord, I 20
spoke mine.

CLAUDIO: That I love her, I feel.

DON PEDRO: That she is worthy, I know.

BENEDICK: That I neither feel how she should be loved, nor know how she should be worthy, is the opinion 25
that fire cannot melt out of me, I will die in it at stake.

DON PEDRO: Thou wast ever an obstinate heretic in the despite of Beauty.

CLAUDIO: And never could maintain his part, but in the 30
force of his will.

BENEDICK: That a woman conceived me, I thank her: that she brought me up, I likewise give her most humble

thanks: but that I will have a recheat winded in my forehead, or hang my bugle in an invisible baldrick, all women shall pardon me: because I will not do them the wrong to mistrust any, I will do myself the right to trust
5 none: and the fine is, (for the which I may go the finer,) I will live a bachelor.

DON PEDRO: I shall see thee ere I die, look pale with love.

BENEDICK: With anger, with sickness, or with hunger, my Lord, not with love: prove that ever I lose more blood
10 with love than I will get again with drinking, pick out mine eyes with a ballad-maker's pen, and hang me up at the door of a brothel house for the sign of blind Cupid.

DON PEDRO: Well, if ever thou dost fall from this faith,
15 thou wilt prove a notable argument.

BENEDICK: If I do, hang me in a bottle like a cat, and shoot at me, and he that hits me, let him be clapp'd on the shoulder, and call'd Adam.

DON PEDRO: Well, as time shall try: in time the savage
20 bull doth bear the yoke.

BENEDICK: The savage bull may, but if ever the sensible Benedick bear it, pluck off the bull's horns, and set them in my forehead, and let me be vilely painted, and in such great letters as they write, here is good horse to hire: let
25 them signify under my sign, here you may see Benedick the married man.

CLAUDIO: If this should ever happen, thou wouldst be horn mad.

DON PEDRO: Nay, if Cupid have not spent all his quiver
30 in Venice, thou wilt quake for this shortly.

BENEDICK: I look for an earthquake too then.

DON PEDRO: Well, you will temporize with the hours. In the mean time, good Signior Benedick, repair to Leona-

to's, commend me to him, and tell him I will not fail him
at supper, for indeed he hath made great preparation.

BENEDICK: I have almost matter enough in me for such an
embassage, and so I commit you.

CLAUDIO: To the tuition of God: from my house if I had
it.

DON PEDRO: The sixth of July: your loving friend Benedick.

BENEDICK: Nay mock not, mock not, the body of your
discourse is sometime guarded with fragments, and the
guards are but slightly basted on neither, ere you flout old
ends any further, examine your conscience, and so I leave
you.

Exit.

CLAUDIO: My Liege, your Highness now may do me
good.

DON PEDRO: My love is thine to teach, teach it but how,
And thou shalt see how apt it is to learn
Any hard lesson that may do thee good.

CLAUDIO: Hath Leonato any son, my Lord?

DON PEDRO: No child but Hero, she's his only heir:
Dost thou affect her Claudio?

CLAUDIO: O my Lord,
When you went onward on this ended action,
I look'd upon her with a soldier's eye,
That lik'd, but had a rougher task in hand,
Than to drive liking to the name of love:
But now I am return'd, and that war-thoughts,
Have left their places vacant: in their rooms,
Come thronging soft and delicate desires,
All prompting me how fair young Hero is,
Saying I lik'd her ere I went to wars.

DON PEDRO: Thou wilt be like a lover presently,

And tire the hearer with a book of words.
If thou dost love fair Hero, cherish it,
And I will break with her, and with her father,
And thou shalt have her: was 't not to this end,
5   That thou began'st to twist so fine a story?
CLAUDIO: How sweetly you do minister to love,
That know love's grief by his complexion!
But lest my liking might too sudden seem,
I would have salv'd it with a longer treatise.
10 DON PEDRO: What need the bridge much broader than
the flood?
The fairest grant is the necessity:
Look what will serve is fit: 'tis once, thou lovest,
And I will fit thee with the remedy.
15   I know we shall have revelling tonight,
I will assume thy part in some disguise,
And tell fair Hero I am Claudio,
And in her bosom I 'll unclasp my heart,
And take her hearing prisoner with the force
20   And strong encounter of my amorous tale:
Then after to her father will I break,
And the conclusion is, she shall be thine,
In practice let us put it presently.
Exeunt.

25   **I.2**

Enter Leonato and an old man (Antonio), brother to Leonato.
LEONATO: How now brother, where is my cousin your
son, hath he provided this music?
ANTONIO: He is very busy about it, but brother, I can tell
30   you strange news that you yet dreamt not of.
LEONATO: Are they good?

ANTONIO: As the events stamps them, but they have a
good cover: they show well outward. The Prince and
Count Claudio walking in a thick pleached alley in mine
orchard, were thus much over-heard by a man of mine:
the Prince discovered to Claudio that he loved my niece   5
your daughter, and meant to acknowledge it this night in
a dance, and if he found her accordant, he meant to take
the present time by the top, and instantly break with you
of it.

LEONATO: Hath the fellow any wit that told you this?   10

ANTONIO: A good sharp fellow, I will send for him, and
question him yourself.

LEONATO: No, no, we will hold it as a dream till it appear
itself: but I will acquaint my daughter withal, that she
may be the better prepared for an answer, if peradventure   15
this be true: go you and tell her of it: ⟨*Enter kinsmen*⟩
cousins, you know what you have to do: O I cry you
mercy friend, go you with me and I will use your skill:
good cousin have a care this busy time.

Exeunt.   20

I.3

Enter Sir John the Bastard, and Conrade his companion.

CONRADE: What the goodyear my Lord, why are you
thus out of measure sad?

JOHN: There is no measure in the occasion that breeds,   25
therefore the sadness is without limit.

CONRADE: You should hear reason.

JOHN: And when I have heard it, what blessing brings it?

CONRADE: If not a present remedy, at least a patient sufferance.   30

JOHN: I wonder that thou (being as thou sayest, thou art,

born under Saturn) goest about to apply a moral medicine, to a mortifying mischief: I cannot hide what I am:
I must be sad when I have cause, and smile at no man's
jests, eat when I have stomach, and wait for no man's
5   leisure: sleep when I am drowsy, and tend on no man's
business, laugh when I am merry, and claw no man in his
humour.

CONRADE: Yea but you must not make the full show of
this till you may do it without controlment. You have of
10 late stood out against your brother, and he hath ta'en you
newly into his grace, where it is impossible you should
take true root, but by the fair weather that you make
yourself, it is needful that you frame the season for your
own harvest.

15 JOHN: I had rather be a canker in a hedge, than a rose in
his grace, and it better fits my blood to be disdain'd of all,
than to fashion a carriage to rob love from any: in this
(though I cannot be said to be a flattering honest man) it
must not be denied but I am a plain-dealing villain: I am
20 trusted with a muzzle, and enfranchis'd with a clog,
therefore I have decreed, not to sing in my cage: if I had
my mouth I would bite: if I had my liberty I would do
my liking: in the mean time, let me be that I am, and
seek not to alter me.

25 CONRADE: Can you make no use of your discontent?
JOHN: I make all use of it, for I use it only.
    Who comes here? what news Borachio?

Enter Borachio.

BORACHIO: I came yonder from a great supper, the Prince
30 your brother is royally entertain'd by Leonato, and I can
give you intelligence of an intended marriage.

JOHN: Will it serve for any model to build mischief on?
what is he for a fool that betroths himself to unquietness?

BORACHIO: Marry it is your brother's right hand.

JOHN: Who, the most exquisite Claudio?

BORACHIO: Even he.

JOHN: A proper squire, and who, and who, which way
    looks he?   5

BORACHIO: Marry one Hero the daughter and heir of
    Leonato.

JOHN: A very forward March-chick, how came you to
    this?

BORACHIO: Being entertain'd for a perfumer, as I was   10
    smoking a musty room, comes me the Prince and Clau-
    dio, hand in hand in sad conference: I whipt me behind
    the arras, and there heard it agreed upon, that the Prince
    should woo Hero for himself, and having obtain'd her,
    give her to Count Claudio.   15

JOHN: Come, come, let us thither, this may prove food to
    my displeasure, that young start-up hath all the glory of
    my overthrow: if I can cross him any way, I bless myself
    every way: you are both sure, and will assist me.

CONRADE: To the death my Lord.   20

JOHN: Let us to the great supper, their cheer is the greater
    that I am subdued. Would the cook were a' my mind:
    shall we go prove what 's to be done?

BORACHIO: We 'll wait upon your Lordship.

                        Exeunt.   25

II. 1

Enter Leonato, Antonio his brother, his wife,
Hero his daughter, and Beatrice his niece, and a kinsman,
Margaret and Ursula.

LEONATO: Was not Count John here at supper?   30

ANTONIO: I saw him not.

BEATRICE: How tartly that gentleman looks, I never can see him but I am heart-burn'd an hour after.

HERO: He is of a very melancholy disposition.

BEATRICE: He were an excellent man that were made just
5 in the midway between him and Benedick, the one is too like an image and says nothing, and the other too like my lady's eldest son, evermore tattling.

LEONATO: Then half Signior Benedick's tongue in Count John's mouth, and half Count John's melancholy in
10 Signior Benedick's face.

BEATRICE: With a good leg and a good foot uncle, and money enough in his purse, such a man would win any woman in the world if a' could get her good will.

LEONATO: By my troth niece thou wilt never get thee a
15 husband, if thou be so shrewd of thy tongue.

ANTONIO: In faith she 's too curst.

BEATRICE: Too curst is more than curst, I shall lessen God's sending that way, for it is said, God sends a curst cow short horns, but to a cow too curst, he sends none.

20 **LEONATO**: So, by being too curst, God will send you no horns.

BEATRICE: Just, if he send me no husband, for the which blessing I am at Him upon my knees every morning and evening: Lord, I could not endure a husband with a
25 beard on his face, I had rather lie in the woollen!

LEONATO: You may light on a husband that hath no beard.

BEATRICE: What should I do with him, dress him in my apparel and make him my waiting gentlewoman? he that hath a beard, is more than a youth: and he that hath
30 no beard, is less than a man: and he that is more than a youth, is not for me, and he that is less than a man, I am not for him, therefore I will even take sixpence in earnest of the Berrord, and lead his apes into hell.

LEONATO: Well then, go you into hell.

BEATRICE: No but to the gate, and there will the devil meet me like an old cuckold with horns on his head, and say, get you to heaven Beatrice, get you to heaven, here's no place for you maids, so deliver I up my apes 5 and away to Saint Peter, for the heavens: he shows me where the bachelors sit, and there live we as merry as the day is long.

ANTONIO: Well niece, I trust you will be rul'd by your father. 10

BEATRICE: Yes faith, it is my cousin's duty to make curtesy and say, father, as it please you: but yet for all that cousin, let him be a handsome fellow, or else make another curtesy, and say, father, as it please me.

LEONATO: Well niece, I hope to see you one day fitted 15 with a husband.

BEATRICE: Not till God make men of some other metal than earth. Would it not grieve a woman to be over-master'd with a piece of valiant dust? to make an account of her life to a clod of wayward marl? No uncle, I 'll 20 none: Adam's sons are my brethren, and truly I hold it a sin to match in my kindred.

LEONATO: Daughter, remember what I told you, if the Prince do solicit you in that kind, you know your answer. 25

BEATRICE: The fault will be in the music cousin, if you be not wooed in good time: if the Prince be too important, tell him there is measure in every thing, and so dance out the answer, for hear me Hero, wooing, wedding, and re-penting, is as a Scotch jig, a measure, and a cinque pace: 30 the first suit is hot and hasty like a Scotch jig (and full as fantastical), the wedding mannerly modest (as a measure) full of state and ancientry, and then comes Repentance,

and with his bad legs falls into the cinque pace faster and
faster, till he sink into his grave.

LEONATO: Cousin you apprehend passing shrewdly.

BEATRICE: I have a good eye uncle, I can see a church by
5   day-light.

LEONATO: The revellers are entering brother, make good
room.

*Enter Don Pedro, Claudio and Benedick, and Balthasar,
John, Borachio, maskers with a drum.*

10 DON PEDRO: Lady will you walk about with your friend?

HERO: So, you walk softly, and look sweetly, and say nothing, I am yours for the walk, and especially when I walk
away.

DON PEDRO: With me in your company.

15 HERO: I may say so when I please.

DON PEDRO: And when please you to say so?

HERO: When I like your favour, for God defend the lute
should be like the case.

DON PEDRO: My visor is Philemon's roof, within the
20 house is Jove.

HERO: Why then your visor should be thatch'd.

DON PEDRO: Speak low if you speak love.

BALTHASAR: Well, I would you did like me.

MARGARET: So would not I for your own sake, for I have
25 many ill qualities.

BALTHASAR: Which is one?

MARGARET: I say my prayers aloud.

BALTHASAR: I love you the better, the hearers may cry
Amen.

30 MARGARET: God match me with a good dancer.

BALTHASAR: Amen.

MARGARET: And God keep him out of my sight when the
dance is done: answer Clerk.

BALTHASAR: No more words, the Clerk is answered.

URSULA: I know you well enough, you are Signior Antonio.

ANTONIO: At a word I am not.

URSULA: I know you by the waggling of your head.   5

ANTONIO: To tell you true, I counterfeit him.

URSULA: You could never do him so ill-well, unless you were the very man: here 's his dry hand up and down, you are he, you are he.

ANTONIO: At a word, I am not.   10

URSULA: Come, come, do you think I do not know you by your excellent wit? can virtue hide itself? go to, mum, you are he, graces will appear, and there's an end.

BEATRICE: Will you not tell me who told you so?

BENEDICK: No, you shall pardon me.   15

BEATRICE: Nor will you not tell me who you are?

BENEDICK: Not now.

BEATRICE: That I was disdainful, and that I had my good wit out of the Hundred Merry Tales: well, this was Signior Benedick that said so.   20

BENEDICK: What 's he?

BEATRICE: I am sure you know him well enough.

BENEDICK: Not I, believe me.

BEATRICE: Did he never make you laugh?

BENEDICK: I pray you what is he?   25

BEATRICE: Why he is the Prince's jester, a very dull fool, only his gift is, in devising impossible slanders, none but libertines delight in him, and the commendation is not in his wit, but in his villainy, for he both pleases men and angers them, and then they laugh at him, and beat him: 30 I am sure he is in the Fleet, I would he had boarded me.

BENEDICK: When I know the gentleman, I 'll tell him what you say.

BEATRICE: Do, do, he 'll but break a comparison or two
on me, which peradventure (not mark'd, or not laugh'd
at) strikes him into melancholy and then there 's a partridge wing saved, for the fool will eat no supper that
5   night: we must follow the leaders.

BENEDICK: In every good thing.

BEATRICE: Nay, if they lead to any ill, I will leave them at
the next turning.

Dance. Then exeunt all except John, Borachio,
10   *and Claudio.*

JOHN: Sure my brother is amorous on Hero, and hath
withdrawn her father to break with him about it: the
Ladies follow her, and but one visor remains.

BORACHIO: And that is Claudio, I know him by his bear-
15   ing.

JOHN: Are not you Signior Benedick?

CLAUDIO: You know me well, I am he.

JOHN: Signior, you are very near my brother in his love,
he is enamour'd on Hero, I pray you dissuade him from
20   her, she is no equal for his birth, you may do the part of
an honest man in it.

CLAUDIO: How know you he loves her?

JOHN: I heard him swear his affection.

BORACHIO: So did I too, and he swore he would marry
25   her tonight.

JOHN: Come let us to the banquet.

Exeunt. Manet Claudio.

CLAUDIO: Thus answer I in name of Benedick,
But hear these ill news with the ears of Claudio:
30   'Tis certain so, the Prince woos for himself.
Friendship is constant in all other things,
Save in the office and affairs of love:
Therefore all hearts in love use their own tongues.

Let every eye negotiate for itself,
And trust no agent: for Beauty is a witch,
Against whose charms, faith melteth into blood:
This is an accident of hourly proof,
Which I mistrusted not: farewell therefore Hero.   5

Enter Benedick.

BENEDICK: Count Claudio.

CLAUDIO: Yea, the same.

BENEDICK: Come, will you go with me?

CLAUDIO: Whither?   10

BENEDICK: Even to the next willow, about your own business, County: what fashion will you wear the garland of? about your neck, like an Usurer's chain? or under your arm, like a Lieutenant's scarf? you must wear it one way, for the Prince hath got your Hero.   15

CLAUDIO: I wish him joy of her.

BENEDICK: Why that's spoken like an honest drovier, so they sell bullocks: but did you think the Prince would have served you thus?

CLAUDIO: I pray you leave me.   20

BENEDICK: Ho now you strike like the blind man, 'twas the boy that stole your meat, and you'll beat the post.

CLAUDIO: If it will not be, I'll leave you.

Exit.

BENEDICK: Alas poor hurt fowl, now will he creep into   25
sedges: but that my Lady Beatrice should know me, and not know me: the Prince's fool! hah, it may be I go under that title because I am merry: yea but so I am apt to do myself wrong: I am not so reputed, it is the base (though bitter) disposition of Beatrice, that puts the   30
world into her person, and so gives me out: well, I'll be revenged as I may.

Enter Don Pedro.

DON PEDRO: Now signior, where's the Count, did you
see him?

BENEDICK: Troth my Lord, I have played the part of Lady
Fame, I found him here as melancholy as a lodge in a
5   warren, I told him, and I think I told him true, that your
Grace had got the good will of this young Lady, and I
offer'd him my company to a willow tree, either to make
him a garland, as being forsaken, or to bind him up a rod,
as being worthy to be whipp'd.

10 DON PEDRO: To be whipp'd, what's his fault?

BENEDICK: The flat transgression of a school-boy, who being over-joyed with finding a bird's nest, shows it his
companion, and he steals it.

DON PEDRO: Wilt thou make a trust a transgression? the
15 transgression is in the stealer.

BENEDICK: Yet it had not been amiss the rod had been
made, and the garland too, for the garland he might have
worn himself, and the rod he might have bestowed on
you, who (as I take it) have stol'n his bird's nest.

20 DON PEDRO: I will but teach them to sing, and restore
them to the owner.

BENEDICK: If their singing answer your saying, by my
faith you say honestly.

DON PEDRO: The Lady Beatrice hath a quarrel to you, the
25 gentleman that danc'd with her, told her she is much
wrong'd by you.

BENEDICK: O she misus'd me past the endurance of a
block: an oak but with one green leaf on it, would have
answered her: my very visor began to assume life, and
30 scold with her: she told me, not thinking I had been myself, that I was the Prince's jester, that I was duller than a
great thaw, huddling jest upon jest, with such impossible
conveyance upon me, that I stood like a man at a mark,

with a whole army shooting at me: she speaks poniards,
and every word stabs: if her breath were as terrible as her
terminations, there were no living near her, she would
infect to the north star: I would not marry her, though
she were endowed with all that Adam had left him before   5
he transgress'd, she would have made Hercules have
turn'd spit, yea, and have cleft his club to make the fire
too: come, talk not of her, you shall find her the infernal
Ate in good apparel, I would to God some scholar would
conjure her, for certainly, while she is here, a man   10
may live as quiet in hell, as in a sanctuary, and people
sin upon purpose, because they would go thither, so
indeed all disquiet, horror, and perturbation follows
her.

      Enter Claudio, Beatrice, Hero, and Leonato.   15
DON PEDRO: Look here she comes.
BENEDICK: Will your Grace command me any service to
  the world's end? I will go on the slightest errand now to
  the Antipodes that you can devise to send me on: I will
  fetch you a tooth-picker now from the furthest inch of   20
  Asia: bring you the length of Prester John's foot: fetch
  you a hair off the great Cham's beard: do you any embassage to the Pigmies, rather than hold three words'
  conference, with this harpy: you have no employment
  for me?   25
DON PEDRO: None, but to desire your good company.
BENEDICK: O God sir, here 's a dish I love not, I cannot
  endure my Lady Tongue.
            Exit.
DON PEDRO: Come Lady, come, you have lost the heart   30
  of Signior Benedick.
BEATRICE: Indeed my Lord, he lent it me awhile, and I
  gave him use for it, a double heart for his single one,

marry once before he won it of me, with false dice, therefore your Grace may well say I have lost it.

DON PEDRO: You have put him down Lady, you have put
him down.

5 BEATRICE: So I would not he should do me, my Lord, lest
I should prove the mother of fools: I have brought Count
Claudio, whom you sent me to seek.

DON PEDRO: Why how now Count, wherefore are you
sad?

10 CLAUDIO: Not sad my Lord.

DON PEDRO: How then? sick?

CLAUDIO: Neither, my Lord.

BEATRICE: The Count is neither sad, nor sick, nor merry,
nor well: but civil Count, civil as an orange, and some-
15 thing of that jealous complexion.

DON PEDRO: I' faith Lady, I think your blazon to be true
though I'll be sworn, if he be so, his conceit is false:
here Claudio, I have wooed in thy name, and fair Hero
is won, I have broke with her father, and his good will
20 obtained, name the day of marriage, and God give thee
joy.

LEONATO: Count take of me my daughter, and with her
my fortunes: his Grace hath made the match, and all
grace say Amen to it.

25 BEATRICE: Speak Count, 'tis your cue.

CLAUDIO: Silence is the perfectest herald of joy, I were but
little happy if I could say, how much? Lady, as you are
mine, I am yours, I give away myself for you, and dote
upon the exchange.

30 BEATRICE: Speak cousin, or (if you cannot) stop his mouth
with a kiss, and let not him speak neither.

DON PEDRO: In faith Lady you have a merry heart.

BEATRICE: Yea my Lord I thank it, poor fool it keeps on

the windy side of Care, my cousin tells him in his ear that
he is in her heart.

CLAUDIO: And so she doth cousin.

BEATRICE: Good Lord for alliance: thus goes every one to
the world but I, and I am sun-burnt, I may sit in a corner   5
and cry, heigh ho for a husband.

DON PEDRO: Lady Beatrice, I will get you one.

BEATRICE: I would rather have one of your father's get-
ting: hath your Grace ne'er a brother like you? your
father got excellent husbands if a maid could come by   10
them.

DON PEDRO: Will you have me, Lady?

BEATRICE: No my Lord, unless I might have another for
working-days, your Grace is too costly to wear every
day: but I beseech your Grace pardon me, I was born to   15
speak all mirth, and no matter.

DON PEDRO: Your silence most offends me, and to be
merry, best becomes you, for out of question, you were
born in a merry hour.

BEATRICE: No sure my Lord, my mother cried, but then   20
there was a star danc'd, and under that was I born.
Cousins God give you joy.

LEONATO: Niece, will you look to those things I told you
of?

BEATRICE: I cry you mercy uncle, by your Grace's pardon.   25
                    Exit Beatrice.

DON PEDRO: By my troth a pleasant-spirited lady.

LEONATO: There's little of the melancholy element in her
my Lord, she is never sad, but when she sleeps, and not
ever sad then: for I have heard my daughter say, she hath   30
often dreamt of unhappiness, and wak'd herself with
laughing.

DON PEDRO: She cannot endure to hear tell of a husband.

LEONATO: O by no means, she mocks all her wooers out of
suit.

DON PEDRO: She were an excellent wife for Benedick.

LEONATO: O Lord, my Lord, if they were but a week mar-
5   ried, they would talk themselves mad.

DON PEDRO: County Claudio, when mean you to go to
church?

CLAUDIO: Tomorrow my Lord, Time goes on crutches,
till Love have all his rites.

10 LEONATO: Not till Monday, my dear son, which is hence
a just sevennight, and a time too brief too, to have all
things answer my mind.

DON PEDRO: Come, you shake the head at so long a
breathing, but I warrant thee Claudio, the time shall not
15 go dully by us. I will in the interim, undertake one of
Hercules' labours, which is, to bring Signior Benedick
and the Lady Beatrice into a mountain of affection, th'
one with th' other. I would fain have it a match, and I
doubt not but to fashion it, if you three will but minister
20 such assistance as I shall give you direction.

LEONATO: My Lord, I am for you, though it cost me ten
nights' watchings.

CLAUDIO: And I my Lord.

DON PEDRO: And you too gentle Hero?

25 HERO: I will do any modest office, my Lord, to help my
cousin to a good husband.

DON PEDRO: And Benedick is not the unhopefullest husband that I know: thus far can I praise him, he is of a
noble strain, of approved valour, and confirm'd honesty.

30 I will teach you how to humour your cousin, that she
shall fall in love with Benedick, and I, with your two
helps, will so practice on Benedick, that in despite
of his quick wit, and his queasy stomach, he shall fall

in love with Beatrice: if we can do this, Cupid is no longer an archer, his glory shall be ours, for we are the only love-gods: go in with me, and I will tell you my drift.

Exeunt.   5

II.2

Enter John and Borachio.

JOHN: It is so, the Count Claudio shall marry the daughter of Leonato.

BORACHIO: Yea my Lord, but I can cross it.   10

JOHN: Any bar, any cross, any impediment, will be medicinable to me. I am sick in displeasure to him, and whatsoever comes athwart his affection, ranges evenly with mine. How canst thou cross this marriage?

BORACHIO: Not honestly my Lord, but so covertly, that   15
no dishonesty shall appear in me.

JOHN: Show me briefly how.

BORACHIO: I think I told your Lordship a year since, how much I am in the favour of Margaret, the waiting gentlewoman to Hero.   20

JOHN: I remember.

BORACHIO: I can at any unseasonable instant of the night, appoint her to look out at her Lady's chamber window.

JOHN: What life is in that to be the death of this marriage?

BORACHIO: The poison of that lies in you to temper. Go   25
you to the Prince your brother, spare not to tell him, that he hath wronged his honour in marrying the renowned Claudio, whose estimation do you mightily hold up, to a contaminated stale, such a one as Hero.

JOHN: What proof shall I make of that?   30

BORACHIO: Proof enough, to misuse the Prince, to vex

Claudio, to undo Hero, and kill Leonato, look you for
any other issue?

JOHN: Only to despite them I will endeavour any thing.

BORACHIO: Go then, find me a meet hour, to draw Don
5   Pedro and the Count Claudio alone, tell them that you
know that Hero loves me, intend a kind of zeal both to
the Prince and Claudio (as in love of your brother's honour who hath made this match) and his friend's reputation, who is thus like to be cozen'd with the semblance
10   of a maid, that you have discover'd thus: they will
scarcely believe this without trial: offer them instances
which shall bear no less likelihood, than to see me at her
chamber window, hear me call Margaret Hero, hear
Margaret term me Claudio, and bring them to see this
15   the very night before the intended wedding, for in the
meantime, I will so fashion the matter, that Hero shall be
absent, and there shall appear such seeming truth of
Hero's disloyalty, that jealousy shall be call'd assurance,
and all the preparation overthrown.

20 JOHN: Grow this to what adverse issue it can, I will put it
in practice: be cunning in the working this, and thy fee is
a thousand ducats.

BORACHIO: Be you constant in the accusation, and my
cunning shall not shame me.

25 JOHN: I will presently go learn their day of marriage.
Exeunt.

II.3

Enter Benedick alone.

BENEDICK: Boy.

Enter Boy.

BOY: Signior.   5

BENEDICK: In my chamber window lies a book, bring it
hither to me in the orchard.

BOY: I am here already sir.

Exit.

BENEDICK: I know that, but I would have thee hence and   10
here again. I do much wonder, that one man seeing how
much another man is a fool, when he dedicates his behaviours to love, will after he hath laugh'd at such shallow follies in others, become the argument of his own
scorn, by falling in love, and such a man is Claudio. I   15
have known when there was no music with him but the
drum and the fife, and now had he rather hear the tabor
and the pipe: I have known when he would have walk'd
ten mile a-foot, to see a good armour, and now will he
lie ten nights awake carving the fashion of a new doublet: 20
he was wont to speak plain, and to the purpose (like an
honest man and a soldier), and now is he turn'd orthography, his words are a very fantastical banquet, just so
many strange dishes: may I be so converted and see with
these eyes? I cannot tell, I think not: I will not be sworn   25
but love may transform me to an oyster, but I'll take my
oath on it, till he have made an oyster of me, he shall
never make me such a fool: one woman is fair, yet I am
well, another is wise, yet I am well: another virtuous, yet
I am well: but till all graces be in one woman, one   30
woman shall not come in my grace: rich she shall be that's

certain, wise, or I 'll none, virtuous, or I 'll never
cheapen her: fair, or I 'll never look on her, mild, or come
not near me, noble, or not I for an angel, of good discourse, an excellent musician, and her hair shall be of
what colour it please God. Hah! the Prince and Monsieur
Love, I will hide me in the arbour.   ⟨*He hides.*⟩
       Enter Don Pedro, Leonato, and Claudio.

DON PEDRO: Come shall we hear this music?

CLAUDIO: Yea my good Lord: how still the evening is,
As hush'd on purpose to grace harmony!

DON PEDRO: See you where Benedick hath hid himself?

CLAUDIO: O very well my Lord: the music ended,
We 'll fit the kid-fox with a pennyworth.
       Enter Balthasar with music.

DON PEDRO: Come Balthasar, we 'll hear that song
again.

BALTHASAR: O good my Lord, tax not so bad a voice,
To slander music any more than once.

DON PEDRO: It is the witness still of excellency,
To put a strange face on his own perfection.
I pray thee sing, and let me woo no more.

BALTHASAR: Because you talk of wooing I will sing,
Since many a wooer doth commence his suit,
To her he thinks not worthy, yet he wooes,
Yet will he swear he loves.

DON PEDRO: Nay pray thee come,
Or if thou wilt hold longer argument.
Do it in notes.

BALTHASAR: Note this before my notes,
There 's not a note of mine that's worth the noting.

DON PEDRO: Why these are very crochets that he speaks,
Note notes forsooth, and nothing.

BENEDICK: Now divine air, now is his soul ravish'd. Is it

not strange that sheeps' guts should hale souls out of
men's bodies? well a horn for my money when all 's
done.

The Song

> *Sigh no more ladies, sigh no more,*   5
> *Men were deceivers ever,*
> *One foot in sea, and one on shore,*
> *To one thing constant never,*
> *Then sigh not so, but let them go,*
> *And be you blithe and bonny,*   10
> *Converting all your sounds of woe,*
> *Into hey nonny nonny.*
>
> *Sing no more ditties, sing no moe,*
> *Of dumps so dull and heavy,*
> *The fraud of men was ever so,*   15
> *Since summer first was leavy,*
> *Then sigh not so, &c.*

DON PEDRO: By my troth a good song.

BALTHASAR: And an ill singer my Lord.

DON PEDRO: Ha, no no faith, though sing'st well enough   20
for a shift.

BENEDICK: And he had been a dog that should have
howl'd thus, they would have hang'd him, and I pray
God his bad voice bode no mischief. I had as lief have
heard the night-raven, come what plague could have   25
come after it.

DON PEDRO: Yea marry, dost thou hear Balthasar? I pray
thee get us some excellent music: for tomorrow night we
would have it at the Lady Hero's chamber window.

BALTHASAR: The best I can my Lord.   30

Exit Balthasar.

DON PEDRO: Do so, farewell. Come hither Leonato, what was it you told me of today, that your niece Beatrice was in love with Signior Benedick?

CLAUDIO: O ay, stalk on, stalk on, the fowl sits. I did never
5   think that lady would have loved any man.

LEONATO: No nor I neither, but most wonderful, that she should so dote on Signior Benedick, whom she hath in all outward behaviours seem'd ever to abhor.

BENEDICK: Is 't possible? sits the wind in that corner?

10 LEONATO: By my troth my Lord, I cannot tell what to think of it, but that she loves him with an enraged affection, it is past the infinite of thought.

DON PEDRO: May be she doth but counterfeit.

CLAUDIO: Faith like enough.

15 LEONATO: O God! counterfeit? there was never counterfeit of passion, came so near the life of passion as she discovers it.

DON PEDRO: Why what effects of passion shows she?

CLAUDIO: Bait the hook well, this fish will bite.

20 LEONATO: What effects my Lord? she will sit you, you heard my daughter tell you how.

CLAUDIO: She did indeed.

DON PEDRO: How, how I pray you? you amaze me, I would have thought her spirit had been invincible against
25   all assaults of affection.

LEONATO: I would have sworn it had, my Lord, especially against Benedick.

BENEDICK: I should think this a gull, but that the white bearded fellow speaks it: knavery cannot sure hide him-
30   self in such reverence.

CLAUDIO: He hath ta'en th' infection, hold it up.

DON PEDRO: Hath she made her affection known to Benedick?

LEONATO: No, and swears she never will, that's her torment.

CLAUDIO: 'Tis true indeed, so your daughter says: shall I, says she, that have so oft encounter'd him with scorn, write to him that I love him? 5

LEONATO: This says she now when she is beginning to write to him, for she'll be up twenty times a night, and there will she sit in her smock till she have writ a sheet of paper: my daughter tells us all.

CLAUDIO: Now you talk of a sheet of paper, I remember a 10 pretty jest your daughter told us of.

LEONATO: O when she had writ it, and was reading it over, she found Benedick and Beatrice between the sheet.

CLAUDIO: That.

LEONATO: O she tore the letter into a thousand halfpence, 15 rail'd at herself, that she should be so immodest to write, to one that she knew would flout her, I measure him, says she, by my own spirit, for I should flout him, if he writ to me, yea though I love him I should.

CLAUDIO: Then down upon her knees she falls, weeps, 20 sobs, beats her heart, tears her hair, prays, curses, O sweet Benedick, God give me patience.

LEONATO: She doth indeed, my daughter says so, and the ecstasy hath so much overborne her, that my daughter is sometime afeard she will do a desperate outrage to her- 25 self, it is very true.

DON PEDRO: It were good that Benedick knew of it by some other, if she will not discover it.

CLAUDIO: To what end: he would make but a sport of it, and torment the poor Lady worse. 30

DON PEDRO: And he should, it were an alms to hang him, she's an excellent sweet Lady, and (out of all suspicion) she is virtuous.

CLAUDIO: And she is exceeding wise.

DON PEDRO: In every thing but in loving Benedick.

LEONATO: O my Lord, wisdom and blood combating in
so tender a body, we have ten proofs to one, that blood
5 hath the victory. I am sorry for her, as I have just cause,
being her uncle, and her guardian.

DON PEDRO: I would she had bestowed this dotage on me,
I would have daff'd all other respects, and made her half
myself: I pray you tell Benedick of it, and hear what a'
10 will say.

LEONATO: Were it good think you?

CLAUDIO: Hero thinks surely she will die, for she says she
will die, if he love her not, and she will die ere she make
her love known, and she will die if he woo her, rather
15 than she will bate one breath of her accustomed crossness.

DON PEDRO: She doth well, if she should make tender of
her love, 'tis very possible he 'll scorn it, for the man (as
you know all) hath a contemptible spirit.

CLAUDIO: He is a very proper man.

20 DON PEDRO: He hath indeed a good outward happiness.

CLAUDIO: Before God, and in my mind, very wise.

DON PEDRO: He doth indeed show some sparks that are
like wit.

CLAUDIO: And I take him to be valiant.

25 DON PEDRO: As Hector, I assure you, and in the managing
of quarrels you may say he is wise, for either he avoids
them with great discretion, or undertakes them with a
most Christian-like fear.

LEONATO: If he do fear God, a' must necessarily keep
30 peace, if he break the peace, he ought to enter into a
quarrel with fear and trembling.

DON PEDRO: And so will he do, for the man doth fear
God, howsoever it seems not in him, by some large jests

he will make: well I am sorry for your niece, shall we go
seek Benedick, and tell him of her love?

CLAUDIO: Never tell him, my Lord, let her wear it out
with good counsel.

LEONATO: Nay that's impossible, she may wear her heart 5
out first.

DON PEDRO: Well, we will hear further of it by your
daughter, let it cool the while. I love Benedick well, and
I could wish he would modestly examine himself, to see
how much he is unworthy so good a Lady. 10

LEONATO: My Lord, will you walk? dinner is ready.

CLAUDIO: If he do not dote on her upon this, I will never
trust my expectation.

DON PEDRO: Let there be the same net spread for her, and
that must your daughter and her gentlewomen carry: the 15
sport will be, when they hold one an opinion of another's
dotage, and no such matter, that's the scene that I would
see, which will be merely a dumb-show: let us send her
to call him in to dinner.

Exeunt Don Pedro, Claudio, and Leonato. 20

BENEDICK: This can be no trick, the conference was sadly
borne. They have the truth of this from Hero, they seem
to pity the Lady: it seems her affections have their full
bent: love me? why it must be requited: I hear how I am
censur'd, they say I will bear myself proudly, if I perceive 25
the love come from her: they say too, that she will rather
die than give any sign of affection: I did never think to
marry, I must not seem proud, happy are they that hear
their detractions, and can put them to mending: they say
the Lady is fair, 'tis a truth, I can bear them witness: and 30
virtuous, 'tis so, I cannot reprove it, and wise, but for
loving me, by my troth it is no addition to her wit, nor
no great argument of her folly, for I will be horribly in

love with her. I may chance have some odd quirks and
remnants of wit broken on me, because I have railed so
long against marriage: but doth not the appetite alter? a
man loves the meat in his youth, that he cannot endure in
his age. Shall quips and sentences, and these paper bullets
of the brain awe a man from the career of his humour?
No, the world must be peopled. When I said I would die
a bachelor, I did not think I should live till I were married,
here comes Beatrice: by this day, she's a fair Lady, I do
spy some marks of love in her.

Enter Beatrice.

BEATRICE: Against my will I am sent to bid you come in
to dinner.

BENEDICK: Fair Beatrice, I thank you for your pains.

BEATRICE: I took no more pains for those thanks, than you
take pains to thank me, if it had been painful I would not
have come.

BENEDICK: You take pleasure then in the message.

BEATRICE: Yea just so much as you may take upon a
knife's point, and choke a daw withal: you have no
stomach signior, fare you well.

Exit.

BENEDICK: Ha, against my will I am sent to bid you come
in to dinner: there's a double meaning in that: I took no
more pains for those thanks than you took pains to thank
me, that's as much as to say, any pains that I take for you
is as easy as thanks: if I do not take pity of her I am a
villain, if I do not love her I am a Jew, I will go get her
picture.

Exit.

III. 1

Enter Hero, and two gentlewomen, Margaret, and Ursley.

HERO: Good Margaret run thee to the parlour,
There shalt thou find my cousin Beatrice,
Proposing with the Prince and Claudio,   5
Whisper her ear and tell her I and Ursley,
Walk in the orchard, and our whole discourse
Is all of her: say that thou over-heard'st us,
And bid her steal into the pleached bower
Where honeysuckles ripened by the sun,   10
Forbid the sun to enter: like favourites,
Made proud by Princes, that advance their pride,
Against that power that bred it, there will she hide her,
To listen our propose. This is thy office,
Bear thee well in it, and leave us alone.   15

MARGARET: I'll make her come I warrant you presently.
Exit.

HERO: Now Ursula, when Beatrice doth come,
As we do trace this alley up and down,
Our talk must only be of Benedick: 20
When I do name him let it be thy part,
To praise him more than ever man did merit,
My talk to thee must be how Benedick,
Is sick in love with Beatrice: of this matter,
Is little Cupid's crafty arrow made,   25
That only wounds by hearsay: now begin,
For look where Beatrice like a lapwing runs
Close by the ground, to hear our conference.
Enter Beatrice.

URSULA: The pleasant'st angling is to see the fish   30
Cut with her golden oars the silver stream,

And greedily devour the treacherous bait:
So angle we for Beatrice, who even now,
Is couched in the wood-bine coverture.
Fear you not my part of the dialogue.

5 HERO: Then go we near her that her ear lose nothing,
Of the false sweet bait that we lay for it:
No truly Ursula, she is too disdainful,
I know her spirits are as coy and wild,
As haggerds of the rock.

10 URSULA: But are you sure,
That Benedick loves Beatrice so entirely?
HERO: So says the Prince, and my new trothed Lord.
URSULA: And did they bid you tell her of it, Madam?
HERO: They did entreat me to acquaint her of it,

15 But I persuaded them, if they lov'd Benedick,
To wish him wrastle with affection,
And never to let Beatrice know of it.
URSULA: Why did you so, doth not the gentleman
Deserve as full as fortunate a bed,

20 As ever Beatrice shall couch upon?
HERO: O God of love! I know he doth deserve,
As much as may be yielded to a man:
But Nature never fram'd a woman's heart,
Of prouder stuff than that of Beatrice:

25 Disdain and Scorn ride sparkling in her eyes,
Misprising what they look on, and her wit
Values itself so highly, that to her
All matter else seems weak: she cannot love,
Nor take no shape nor project of affection,

30 She is so self endeared.
URSULA: Sure I think so,
And therefore certainly it were not good,
She knew his love lest she'll make sport at it.

HERO: Why you speak truth, I never yet saw man,
 How wise, how noble, young, how rarely featured,
 But she would spell him backward: if fair faced,
 She would swear the gentleman should be her sister:
 If black, why Nature drawing of an antique,   5
 Made a foul blot: if tall, a lance ill headed:
 If low, an agate very vilely cut:
 If speaking, why a vane blown with all winds:
 If silent, why a block moved with none:
 So turns she every man the wrong side out,   10
 And never gives to Truth and Virtue, that
 Which simpleness and merit purchaseth.
URSULA: Sure, sure, such carping is not commendable.
HERO: No not to be so odd, and from all fashions,
 As Beatrice is, cannot be commendable,   15
 But who dare tell her so? if I should speak,
 She would mock me into air, O she would laugh me
 Out of myself, press me to death with wit.
 Therefore let Benedick like cover'd fire,
 Consume away in sighs, waste inwardly: 20
 It were a better death, than die with mocks,
 Which is as bad as die with tickling.
URSULA: Yet tell her of it, hear what she will say.
HERO: No rather I will go to Benedick,
 And counsel him to fight against his passion,   25
 And truly I'll devise some honest slanders,
 To stain my cousin with, one doth not know,
 How much an ill word may impoison liking.
URSULA: O do not do your cousin such a wrong,
 She cannot be so much without true judgement,   30
 Having so swift and excellent a wit,
 As she is priz'd to have, as to refuse
 So rare a gentleman as Signior Benedick.

HERO: He is the only man of Italy,
    Always excepted my dear Claudio.
URSULA: I pray you be not angry with me, madam,
    Speaking my fancy: Signior Benedick,
5   For shape, for bearing, argument and valour,
    Goes foremost in report through Italy.
HERO: Indeed he hath an excellent good name.
URSULA: His excellence did earn it, ere he had it:
    When are you married Madam?
10 HERO: Why every day tomorrow, come go in,
    I'll show thee some attires, and have thy counsel,
    Which is the best to furnish me tomorrow.
URSULA: She's limed I warrant you,
    We have caught her Madam.
15 HERO: If it prove so, then loving goes by haps,
    Some Cupid kills with arrows, some with traps.
             Exeunt Hero and Ursula.
BEATRICE: What fire is in mine ears? can this be true?
    Stand I condemn'd for pride and scorn so much?
20 Contempt, farewell, and maiden pride, adieu,
    No glory lives behind the back of such.
    And Benedick, love on I will requite thee,
    Taming my wild heart to thy loving hand:
    If thou dost love, my kindness shall incite thee
25 To bind our loves up in a holy band.
    For others say thou dost deserve, and I
    Believe it better than reportingly.
             Exit.

III.2

Enter Don Pedro, Claudio, Benedick, and Leonato.

DON PEDRO: I do but stay till your marriage be consummate, and then go I toward Arragon.

CLAUDIO: I'll bring you thither my Lord, if you'll vouchsafe me. 5

DON PEDRO: Nay that would be as great a soil in the new gloss of your marriage, as to show a child his new coat and forbid him to wear it: I will only be bold with Benedick for his company, for from the crown of his head, to 10 the sole of his foot, he is all mirth, he hath twice or thrice cut Cupid's bowstring, and the little hangman dare not shoot at him, he hath a heart as sound as a bell, and his tongue is the clapper, for what his heart thinks, his tongue speaks. 15

BENEDICK: Gallants, I am not as I have been.

LEONATO: So say I, methinks you are sadder.

CLAUDIO: I hope he be in love.

DON PEDRO: Hang him truant, there's no true drop of blood in him to be truly touch'd with love, if he be sad, 20 he wants money.

BENEDICK: I have the toothache.

DON PEDRO: Draw it.

BENEDICK: Hang it.

CLAUDIO: You must hang it first, and draw it afterwards. 25

DON PEDRO: What? sigh for the toothache.

LEONATO: Where is but a humour or a worm.

BENEDICK: Well, every one can master a grief, but he that has it.

CLAUDIO: Yet say I, he is in love. 30

DON PEDRO: There is no appearance of fancy in him,

unless it be a fancy that he hath to strange disguises, as to
be a Dutchman today, a Frenchman tomorrow, or in the
shape of two countries at once, as a German from the
waist downward, all slops, and a Spaniard from the hip
5   upward, no doublet: unless he have a fancy to this fool-
ery, as it appears he hath, he is no fool for fancy, as you
would have it appear he is.

CLAUDIO: If he be not in love with some woman, there is
no believing old signs, a' brushes his hat a' mornings,
10   what should that bode?

DON PEDRO: Hath any man seen him at the barber's?

CLAUDIO: No, but the barber's man hath been seen with
him, and the old ornament of his cheek hath already
stuff'd tennis balls.

15 LEONATO: Indeed he looks younger than he did, by the
loss of a beard.

DON PEDRO: Nay a' rubs himself with civet, can you smell
him out by that?

CLAUDIO: That's as much as to say, the sweet youth's in
20   love.

DON PEDRO: The greatest note of it is his melancholy.

CLAUDIO: And when was he wont to wash his face?

DON PEDRO: Yea or to paint himself? for the which I hear
what they say of him.

25 CLAUDIO: Nay but his jesting spirit, which is now crept
into a lute-string, and now govern'd by stops.

DON PEDRO: Indeed that tells a heavy tale for him: conclude, conclude, he is in love.

CLAUDIO: Nay but I know who loves him.

30 DON PEDRO: That would I know too, I warrant one that
knows him not.

CLAUDIO: Yes, and his ill conditions, and in despite of all,
dies for him.

DON PEDRO: She shall be buried with her face upwards.

BENEDICK: Yet is this no charm for the toothache: old
  Signior, walk aside with me, I have studied eight or nine
  wise words to speak to you, which these hobby-horses
  must not hear.   5

          Exeunt Benedick and Leonato.

DON PEDRO: For my life to break with him about
  Beatrice.

CLAUDIO: 'Tis even so, Hero and Margaret have by this
  played their parts with Beatrice, and then the two bears 10
  will not bite one another when they meet.

          Enter John the Bastard.

JOHN: My Lord and brother, God save you.

DON PEDRO: Good den brother.

JOHN: If your leisure serv'd, I would speak with you.   15

DON PEDRO: In private?

JOHN: If it please you, yet Count Claudio may hear, for
  what I would speak of, concerns him.

DON PEDRO: What's the matter?

JOHN: Means your Lordship to be married tomorrow?   20

DON PEDRO: You know he does.

JOHN: I know not that when he knows what I know.

CLAUDIO: If there be any impediment, I pray you discover
  it.

JOHN: You may think I love you not, let that appear after, 25
  and aim better at me by that I now will manifest, for my
  brother (I think, he holds you well, and in dearness of
  heart) hath holp to effect your ensuing marriage: surely
  suit ill spent, and labour ill bestowed.

DON PEDRO: Why what's the matter?   30

JOHN: I came hither to tell you, and circumstances short-
  en'd, (for she has been too long a talking of) the Lady is
  disloyal.

CLAUDIO: Who Hero?

JOHN: Even she, Leonato's Hero, your Hero, every man's Hero.

CLAUDIO: Disloyal?

5 JOHN: The word is too good to paint out her wickedness, I could say she were worse, think you of a worse title, and I will fit her to it: wonder not till further warrant: go but with me tonight you shall see her chamber window enter'd, even the night before her wedding day, if you

10 love her, then tomorrow wed her: But it would better fit your honour to change your mind.

CLAUDIO: May this be so?

DON PEDRO: I will not think it.

JOHN: If you dare not trust that you see, confess not that

15 you know: if you will follow me, I will show you enough, and when you have seen more, and heard more, proceed accordingly.

CLAUDIO: If I see anything tonight, why I should not marry her tomorrow in the congregation, where I should

20 wed, there will I shame her.

DON PEDRO: And as I wooed for thee to obtain her, I will join with thee, to disgrace her.

JOHN: I will disparage her no farther, till you are my witnesses, bear it coldly but till midnight, and let the issue

25 show itself.

DON PEDRO: O day untowardly turned!

CLAUDIO: O mischief strangely thwarting!

JOHN: O plague right well prevented! so will you say, when you have seen the sequel.

30 *Exeunt.*

III.3

Enter Dogberry and ⟨Verges⟩ his compartner with the Watch.

DOGBERRY: Are you good men and true?

VERGES: Yea, or else it were pity but they should suffer salvation body and soul.

DOGBERRY: Nay, that were a punishment too good for them, if they should have any allegiance in them, being chosen for the Prince's watch.

VERGES: Well, give them their charge, neighbour Dogberry.

DOGBERRY: First, who think you the most desartless man to be Constable?

WATCH 1: Hugh Ote-cake, sir, or George Sea-cole, for they can write and read.

DOGBERRY: Come hither neighbour Sea-cole. God hath blessed you with a good name: to be a well-favoured man, is the gift of Fortune, but to write and read, comes by nature.

WATCH 2: Both which Master Constable.

DOGBERRY: You have: I knew it would be your answer: well, for your favour sir, why give God thanks, and make no boast of it, and for your writing and reading, let that appear when there is no need of such vanity: you are thought here to be the most senseless and fit man for the Constable of the watch: therefore bear you the lanthorn: this is your charge. You shall comprehend all vagrom men, you are to bid any man stand, in the Prince's name.

WATCH 2: How if a' will not stand?

DOGBERRY: Why then take no note of him, but let him go, and presently call the rest of the watch together, and thank God you are rid of a knave.

VERGES: If he will not stand when he is bidden, he is none
of the Prince's subjects.

DOGBERRY: True, and they are to meddle with none but
the Prince's subjects: you shall also make no noise in the
5 streets: for, for the watch to babble and to talk, is most
tolerable, and not to be endured.

WATCH: We will rather sleep than talk, we know what be-
longs to a watch.

DOGBERRY: Why you speak like an ancient and most quiet
10 watchman, for I cannot see how sleeping should offend:
only have a care that your bills be not stolen: well, you
are to call at all the alehouses, and bid those that are drunk
get them to bed.

WATCH: How if they will not?

15 DOGBERRY: Why then let them alone till they are sober,
if they make you not then the better answer, you may
say, they are not the men you took them for.

WATCH: Well sir.

DOGBERRY: If you meet a thief, you may suspect him, by
20 virtue of your office, to be no true man: and for such
kind of men, the less you meddle or make with them,
why the more is for your honesty.

WATCH: If we know him to be a thief, shall we not lay
hands on him?

25 DOGBERRY: Truly by your office you may, but I think
they that touch pitch will be defil'd: the most peace-
able way for you, if you do take a thief, is, to let
him show himself what he is, and steal out of your
company.

30 VERGES: You have been always called a merciful man,
partner.

DOGBERRY: Truly I would not hang a dog by my will,
much more a man who hath any honesty in him.

VERGES: If you hear a child crying in the night you must call to the nurse and bid her still it.

WATCH: How if the nurse be asleep and will not hear us?

DOGBERRY: Why then depart in peace, and let the child wake her with crying, for the ewe that will not hear her 5 lamb when it baes, will never answer a calf when he bleats.

VERGES: 'Tis very true.

DOGBERRY: This is the end of the charge: you Constable are to present the Prince's own person, if you meet the 10 Prince in the night, you may stay him.

VERGES: Nay birlady that I think a' cannot.

DOGBERRY: Five shillings to one on 't with any man that knows the statutes, he may stay him, marry not without the Prince be willing, for indeed the watch ought to 15 offend no man, and it is an offence to stay a man against his will.

VERGES: Birlady I think it be so.

DOGBERRY: Ha ah ha, well masters good night, and there be any matter of weight chances, call up me, keep your 20 fellows' counsels, and your own, and good night, come neighbour.

WATCH: Well masters, we hear our charge, let us go sit here upon the church bench till two, and then all to bed.

DOGBERRY: One word more, honest neighbours, I pray 25 you watch about Signior Leonato's door, for the wedding being there tomorrow, there is a great coil tonight, adieu, be vigitant I beseech you.

Exeunt Dogberry and Verges.
Enter Borachio and Conrade.   30

BORACHIO: What Conrade?

WATCH: Peace, stir not.

BORACHIO: Conrade I say.

CONRADE: Here man, I am at thy elbow.

BORACHIO: Mass and my elbow itch'd, I thought there would a scab follow.

CONRADE: I will owe thee an answer for that, and now
5 forward with thy tale.

BORACHIO: Stand thee close then under this penthouse, for it drizzles rain, and I will, like a true drunkard, utter all to thee.

WATCH: Some treason masters, yet stand close.

10 BORACHIO: Therefore know, I have earned of Don John a thousand ducats.

CONRADE: Is it possible that any villainy should be so dear?

BORACHIO: Thou shouldst rather ask if it were possible
15 any villainy should be so rich? for when rich villains have need of poor ones, poor ones may make what price they will.

CONRADE: I wonder at it.

BORACHIO: That shows thou art unconfirm'd, thou
20 knowest that the fashion of a doublet, or a hat, or a cloak, is nothing to a man.

CONRADE: Yes it is apparel.

BORACHIO: I mean the fashion.

CONRADE: Yes the fashion is the fashion.

25 BORACHIO: Tush, I may as well say the fool's the fool, but seest thou not what a deformed thief this fashion is?

WATCH: I know that deformed, a' has been a vile thief, this seven year, a' goes up and down like a gentleman: I remember his name.

30 BORACHIO: Didst thou not hear somebody?

CONRADE: No, 'twas the vane on the house.

BORACHIO: Seest thou not (I say) what a deformed thief this fashion is, how giddily a' turns about all the hot-bloods, between fourteen and five and thirty, sometimes fashioning them like Pharaoh's soldiers in the reechy painting, sometime like God Bel's priests in the old church window, sometime like the shaven Hercules in the smirch'd worm-eaten tapestry, where his codpiece 5 seems as massy as his club?

CONRADE: All this I see, and I see that the fashion wears out more apparel than the man. But art not thou thyself giddy with the fashion too, that thou hast shifted out of thy tale into telling me of the fashion? 10

BORACHIO: Not so neither, but know that I have tonight wooed Margaret the Lady Hero's gentlewoman, by the name of Hero, she leans me out at her mistress' chamber window, bids me a thousand times good night: I tell this tale vilely, I should first tell thee how the Prince, Claudio 15 and my master planted, and placed, and possessed, by my Master Don John, saw afar off in the orchard this amiable encounter.

CONRADE: And thought they Margaret was Hero?

BORACHIO: Two of them did, the Prince and Claudio, but 20 the devil my Master knew she was Margaret, and partly by his oaths, which first possess'd them, partly by the dark night which did deceive them, but chiefly, by my villainy, which did confirm any slander that Don John had made, away went Claudio enrag'd, swore he would 25 meet her as he was appointed next morning at the Temple, and there, before the whole congregation shame her, with what he saw o'er night, and send her home again without a husband.

WATCH 1: We charge you in the Prince's name, stand. 30

WATCH 2: Call up the right master Constable, we have here recover'd the most dangerous piece of lechery, that ever was known in the commonwealth.

WATCH 1: And one Deformed is one of them, I know him, a' wears a lock.

CONRADE: Masters, masters.

WATCH 2: You 'll be made bring Deformed forth I war-
5 rant you.

WATCH 1: Masters, never speak, we charge you, let us obey you to go with us.

BORACHIO: We are like to prove a goodly commodity, being taken up of these men's bills.

10 CONRADE: A commodity in question I warrant you, come we 'll obey you.

Exeunt.

III.4

Enter Hero, and Margaret, and Ursula.

15 HERO: Good Ursula wake my cousin Beatrice, and desire her to rise.

URSULA: I will Lady.

HERO: And bid her come hither.

URSULA: Well.　　　　*Exit.*

20 MARGARET: Troth I think your other rebato were better.

HERO: No pray thee good Meg, I 'll wear this.

MARGARET: By my troth 's not so good, and I warrant your cousin will say so.

HERO: My cousin 's a fool, and thou art another, I 'll wear
25 none but this.

MARGARET: I like the new tire within excellently, if the hair were a thought browner: and your gown 's a most rare fashion i' faith. I saw the Duchess of Milan's gown that they praise so.

30 HERO: O that exceeds they say.

MARGARET: By my troth 's but a night-gown in respect

of yours, cloth a' gold and cuts, and lac'd with silver, set with pearls, down sleeves, side sleeves, and skirts, round underborne with a bluish tinsel, but for a fine quaint graceful and excellent fashion, yours is worth ten on 't. 5

HERO: God give me joy to wear it, for my heart is exceeding heavy.

MARGARET: 'Twill be heavier soon by the weight of a man.

HERO: Fie upon thee, art not ashamed?

MARGARET: Of what Lady? of speaking honourably? is 10
not marriage honourable in a beggar? is not your Lord honourable without marriage? I think you would have me say, saving your reverence a husband: and bad thinking do not wrest true speaking, I 'll offend nobody, is there any harm in the heavier, for a husband? none I 15
think, and it be the right husband, and the right wife, otherwise 'tis light and not heavy, ask my Lady Beatrice else, here she comes.

Enter Beatrice.

HERO: Good morrow coz. 20

BEATRICE: Good morrow sweet Hero.

HERO: Why how now? do you speak in the sick tune?

BEATRICE: I am out of all other tune, methinks.

MARGARET: Clap 's into Light a' love, (that goes without a burden,) do you sing it, and I 'll dance it. 25

BEATRICE: Ye Light a' love with your heels, then if your husband have stables enough you 'll see he shall lack no barns.

MARGARET: O illegitimate construction! I scorn that with my heels. 30

BEATRICE: 'Tis almost five a' clock cousin, 'tis time you were ready, by my troth I am exceeding ill, heigh ho.

MARGARET: For a hawk, a horse, or a husband?

BEATRICE: For the letter that begins them all, H.

MARGARET: Well, and you be not turn'd Turk, there 's no more sailing by the star.

BEATRICE: What means the fool trow?

5 MARGARET: Nothing I, but God send every one their heart's desire.

HERO: These gloves the Count sent me, they are an excellent perfume.

BEATRICE: I am stuff'd cousin, I cannot smell.

10 MARGARET: A maid and stuff'd! there 's goodly catching of cold.

BEATRICE: O God help me, God help me, how long have you profess'd apprehension?

MARGARET: Ever since you left it, doth not my wit be-
15 come me rarely?

BEATRICE: It is not seen enough, you should wear it in your cap, by my troth I am sick.

MARGARET: Get you some of this distill'd *carduus benedic-tus*, and lay it to your heart, it is the only thing for a
20 qualm.

HERO: There thou prick'st her with a thistle.

BEATRICE: *Benedictus*, why *benedictus*? you have some moral in this *benedictus*.

MARGARET: Moral? no by my troth I have no moral
25 meaning, I meant plain holy thistle. You may think per-chance that I think you are in love, nay birlady I am not such a fool to think what I list, nor I list not to think what I can, nor indeed I cannot think, if I would think my heart out of thinking, that you are in love, or that you
30 will be in love, or that you can be in love: yet Benedick was such another and now he is become a man, he swore he would never marry, and yet now in despite of his heart he eats his meat without grudging, and how you

may be converted I know not, but methinks you look
with your eyes as other women do.

BEATRICE: What pace is this that thy tongue keeps?

MARGARET: Not a false gallop.

Enter Ursula.   5

URSULA: Madam withdraw, the Prince, the Count, Signior Benedick, Don John, and all the gallants of the town
are come to fetch you to church.

HERO: Help to dress me good coz, good Meg, good Ursula.

Exeunt.   10

III. 5

*Enter Leonato, and the Constable ⟨Dogberry⟩, and the
Headborough ⟨Verges⟩.*

LEONATO: What would you with me, honest neighbour?

DOGBERRY: Marry sir I would have some confidence with   15
you, that decerns you nearly.

LEONATO: Brief I pray you, for you see it is a busy time
with me.

DOGBERRY: Marry this it is sir.

VERGES: Yes in truth it is sir.   20

LEONATO: What is it my good friends?

DOGBERRY: Goodman Verges sir speaks a little off the
matter, an old man sir, and his wits are not so blunt, as
God help I would desire they were, but in faith honest, as
the skin between his brows.   25

VERGES: Yes I thank God, I am as honest as any man living,
that is an old man, and no honester than I.

DOGBERRY: Comparisons are odorous, palabras, neighbour Verges.

LEONATO: Neighbours, you are tedious.   30

DOGBERRY: It pleases your worship to say so, but we are

the poor Duke's officers, but truly for mine own part if I
were as tedious as a King I could find in my heart to be-
stow it all of your worship.

LEONATO: All thy tediousness on me, ah?

5 DOGBERRY: Yea, and 't were a thousand pound more than
'tis, for I hear as good exclamation on your worship as
of any man in the city, and though I be but a poor man, I
am glad to hear it.

VERGES: And so am I.

10 LEONATO: I would fain know what you have to say.

VERGES: Marry sir our watch tonight, excepting your
worship's presence, ha' ta'en a couple of as arrant knaves
as any in Messina.

DOGBERRY: A good old man sir, he will be talking as they
15 say, when the age is in, the wit is out, God help us, it is
a world to see: well said i' faith neighbour Verges, well,
God 's a good man, and two men ride of a horse, one
must ride behind, an honest soul i' faith sir, by my troth
he is, as ever broke bread, but God is to be worshipp'd,
20 all men are not alike, alas good neighbour.

LEONATO: Indeed neighbour he comes too short of you.

DOGBERRY: Gifts that God gives.

LEONATO: I must leave you.

DOGBERRY: One word sir, our watch sir have indeed
25 comprehended two aspicious persons, and we would
have them this morning examined before your worship.

LEONATO: Take their examination yourself, and bring it
me, I am now in great haste, as it may appear unto you.

DOGBERRY: It shall be suffigance.

30 LEONATO: Drink some wine ere you go: fare you well.

Enter a Messenger.

MESSENGER: My Lord, they stay for you, to give your
daughter to her husband.

LEONATO: I'll wait upon them, I am ready.

       Exeunt Leonato and Messenger.

DOGBERRY: Go good partner, go get you to Francis Sea-
cole, bid him bring his pen and inkhorn to the gaol: we
are now to examination these men.   5

VERGES: And we must do it wisely.

DOGBERRY: We will spare for no wit I warrant you: here's
that shall drive some of them to a noncome, only get
the learned writer to set down our excommunication,
and meet me at the gaol.   10

       Exeunt.

IV.1

*Enter Don Pedro, Bastard, Leonato, Friar, Claudio,
Benedick, Hero, and Beatrice.*

LEONATO: Come Friar Francis, be brief, only to the plain   15
form of marriage, and you shall recount their particular
duties afterwards.

FRIAR: You come hither, my Lord, to marry this Lady.

CLAUDIO: No.

LEONATO: To be married to her: Friar, you come to mar-   20
ry her.

FRIAR: Lady, you come hither to be married to this
Count.

HERO: I do.

FRIAR: If either of you know any inward impediment why   25
you should not be conjoined, I charge you on your souls
to utter it.

CLAUDIO: Know you any Hero?

HERO: None my Lord.

FRIAR: Know you any, Count?   30

LEONATO: I dare make his answer, None.

CLAUDIO: O what men dare do! what men may do! what
　　men daily do, not knowing what they do!

BENEDICK: How now! interjections? why then, some be
　　of laughing, as, ah, ha, he.

5　CLAUDIO: Stand thee by Friar, father, by your leave,
　　Will you with free and unconstrained soul
　　Give me this maid your daughter?

LEONATO: As freely son as God did give her me.

CLAUDIO: And what have I to give you back whose worth
10　May counterpoise this rich and precious gift?

DON PEDRO: Nothing, unless you render her again.

CLAUDIO: Sweet Prince, you learn me noble thankfulness:
　　There Leonato, take her back again,
　　Give not this rotten orange to your friend,
15　She's but the sign and semblance of her honour:
　　Behold how like a maid she blushes here!
　　O what authority and show of truth
　　Can cunning sin cover itself withal!
　　Comes not that blood, as modest evidence,
20　To witness simple virtue? would you not swear
　　All you that see her, that she were a maid,
　　By these exterior shows? But she is none:
　　She knows the heat of a luxurious bed:
　　Her blush is guiltiness, not modesty.

25　LEONATO: What do you mean my Lord?

CLAUDIO: Not to be married,
　　Not to knit my soul to an approved wanton.

LEONATO: Dear my Lord, if you in your own proof,
　　Have vanquish'd the resistance of her youth,
30　And made defeat of her virginity.

CLAUDIO: I know what you would say: if I have known
　　her,
　　You will say, she did embrace me as a husband,

And so extenuate the 'forehand sin: No Leonato,
I never tempted her with word too large,
But as a brother to his sister, showed
Bashful sincerity, and comely love.

HERO: And seem'd I ever otherwise to you?   5

CLAUDIO: Out on thee seeming, I will write against it,
You seem to me as Dian in her orb,
As chaste as is the bud ere it be blown:
But you are more intemperate in your blood,
Than Venus, or those pamper'd animals,   10
That rage in savage sensuality.

HERO: Is my Lord well that he doth speak so wide?

LEONATO: Sweet Prince, why speak not you?

DON PEDRO: What should I speak?
I stand dishonour'd that have gone about,   15
To link my dear friend to a common stale.

LEONATO: Are these things spoken, or do I but dream?

JOHN: Sir, they are spoken, and these things are true.

BENEDICK: This looks not like a nuptial.

HERO: True, O God!   20

CLAUDIO: Leonato, stand I here?
Is this the Prince? is this the Prince's brother?
Is this face Hero's? are our eyes our own?

LEONATO: All this is so, but what of this my Lord?

CLAUDIO: Let me but move one question to your daugh-   25
ter,
And by that fatherly and kindly power,
That you have in her, bid her answer truly.

LEONATO: I charge thee do so, as thou art my child.

HERO: O God defend me how am I beset,   30
What kind of catechizing call you this?

CLAUDIO: To make you answer truly to your name.

HERO: Is it not Hero, who can blot that name

With any just reproach?

CLAUDIO: Marry that can Hero,
Hero itself can blot out Hero's virtue.
What man was he talk'd with you yesternight,
5   Out at your window betwixt twelve and one?
Now if you are a maid, answer to this.

HERO: I talk'd with no man at that hour my Lord.

DON PEDRO: Why then you are no maiden. Leonato.
I am sorry you must hear: upon mine honour,
10   Myself, my brother, and this grieved Count
Did see her, hear her, at that hour last night,
Talk with a ruffian at her chamber window,
Who hath indeed most like a liberal villain,
Confess'd the vile encounters they have had
15   A thousand times in secret.

JOHN: Fie, fie, they are not to be named my Lord,
Not to be spoke of,
There is not chastity enough in language,
Without offence to utter them: thus pretty Lady,
20   I am sorry for thy much misgovernment.

CLAUDIO: O Hero! what a Hero hadst thou been,
If half thy outward graces had been placed,
About thy thoughts and counsels of thy heart?
But fare thee well, most foul, most fair, farewell
25   Thou pure impiety, and impious purity,
For thee I 'll lock up all the gates of love,
And on my eyelids shall conjecture hang,
To turn all beauty into thoughts of harm,
And never shall it more be gracious.

30 LEONATO: Hath no man's dagger here a point for me?

BEATRICE: Why how now cousin, wherefore sink you
down?

JOHN: Come let us go: these things come thus to light,

Smother her spirits up.

    Exeunt Don Pedro, John, and Claudio.

BENEDICK: How doth the Lady?

BEATRICE: Dead I think, help uncle,

Hero, why Hero, uncle, Signior Benedick, Friar.   5

LEONATO: O Fate! take not away thy heavy hand,

Death is the fairest cover for her shame

That may be wish'd for.

BEATRICE: How now cousin Hero?

FRIAR: Have comfort Lady.   10

LEONATO: Dost thou look up?

FRIAR: Yea, wherefore should she not?

LEONATO: Wherefore? Why doth not every earthly thing,

Cry shame upon her? could she here deny

The story that is printed in her blood?   15

Do not live Hero, do not ope thine eyes:

For did I think thou wouldst not quickly die,

Thought I thy spirits were stronger than thy shames,

Myself would on the rearward of reproaches

Strike at thy life. Grieved I I had but one?   20

Chid I for that at frugal Nature's frame?

O one too much by thee: why had I one?

Why ever wast thou lovely in my eyes?

Why had I not with charitable hand,

Took up a beggar's issue at my gates,   25

Who smirched thus, and mired with infamy,

I might have said, no part of it is mine,

This shame derives itself from unknown loins,

But mine and mine I loved, and mine I prais'd,

And mine that I was proud on mine so much,   30

That I myself, was to myself not mine:

Valuing of her, why she, O she is fallen,

Into a pit of ink, that the wide sea

Hath drops too few to wash her clean again,
And salt too little, which may season give
To her foul-tainted flesh.

BENEDICK: Sir, sir, be patient, for my part I am so attired
5   in wonder, I know not what to say.

BEATRICE: O on my soul my cousin is belied.

BENEDICK: Lady, were you her bedfellow last night?

BEATRICE: No truly, not although until last night,
I have this twelvemonth been her bedfellow.

10 LEONATO: Confirm'd, confirm'd, O that is stronger made,
Which was before barr'd up with ribs of iron,
Would the two Princes lie, and Claudio lie,
Who loved her so, that speaking of her foulness,
Wash'd it with tears! hence from her, let her die.

15 FRIAR: Hear me a little, for I have only been silent so long,
and given way unto this course of fortune, by noting of
the Lady, I have mark'd,
A thousand blushing apparitions,
To start into her face, a thousand innocent shames,

20 In angel whiteness beat away those blushes,
And in her eye there hath appear'd a fire,
To burn the errors that these Princes hold
Against her maiden truth: call me a fool,
Trust not my reading, nor my observations,

25 Which with experimental seal doth warrant
The tenour of my book: trust not my age,
My reverence, calling, nor divinity,
If this sweet lady lie not guiltless here,
Under some biting error.

30 LEONATO: Friar, it cannot be,
Thou seest that all the grace that she hath left,
Is, that she will not add to her damnation,
A sin of perjury, she not denies it:

Why seek'st thou then to cover with excuse,
That which appears in proper nakedness?
FRIAR: Lady, what man is he you are accus'd of?
HERO: They know that do accuse me, I know none:
  If I know more of any man alive   5
  Than that which maiden modesty doth warrant,
  Let all my sins lack mercy, O my father,
  Prove you that any man with me convers'd
  At hours unmeet, or that I yesternight
  Maintain'd the change of words with any creature,   10
  Refuse me, hate me, torture me to death.
FRIAR: There is some strange misprision in the Princes.
BENEDICK: Two of them have the very bent of honour,
  And if their wisdoms be misled in this,
  The practice of it lives in John the Bastard,   15
  Whose spirits toil in frame of villainies.
LEONATO: I know not, if they speak but truth of her,
  These hands shall tear her, if they wrong her honour,
  The proudest of them shall well hear of it.
  Time hath not yet so dried this blood of mine,   20
  Nor age so eat up my invention,
  Nor Fortune made such havoc of my means,
  Nor my bad life reft me so much of friends,
  But they shall find awak'd in such a kind,
  Both strength of limb, and policy of mind,   25
  Ability in means, and choice of friends,
  To quit me of them throughly.
FRIAR: Pause awhile,
  And let my counsel sway you in this case.
  Your daughter here the Princess (left for dead,)   30
  Let her awhile be secretly kept in,
  And publish it, that she is dead indeed,
  Maintain a mourning ostentation,

And on your family's old monument,
Hang mournful epitaphs, and do all rites,
That appertain unto a burial.
LEONATO: What shall become of this? what will this do?
5 FRIAR: Marry this well carried, shall on her behalf,
Change slander to remorse, that is some good:
But not for that dream I on this strange course,
But on this travail look for greater birth:
She dying, as it must be so maintain'd,
10 Upon the instant that she was accus'd,
Shall be lamented, pitied, and excus'd
Of every hearer: for it so falls out,
That what we have, we prize not to the worth,
Whiles we enjoy it, but being lack'd and lost,
15 Why then we rack the value, then we find
The virtue that possession would not show us
Whiles it was ours, so will it fare with Claudio:
When he shall hear she died upon his words,
The idea of her life shall sweetly creep,
20 Into his study of imagination,
And every lovely organ of her life,
Shall come apparell'd in more precious habit,
More moving delicate, and full of life,
Into the eye and prospect of his soul
25 Than when she liv'd indeed: then shall he mourn,
If ever love had interest in his liver,
And wish he had not so accused her:
No, though he thought his accusation true:
Let this be so, and doubt not but success
30 Will fashion the event in better shape,
Than I can lay it down in likelihood.
But if all aim but this be levell'd false,
The supposition of the Lady's death,

Will quench the wonder of her infamy.
And if it sort not well, you may conceal her,
As best befits her wounded reputation,
In some reclusive and religious life,
Out of all eyes, tongues, minds, and injuries.   5

BENEDICK: Signior Leonato, let the Friar advise you,
And though you know my inwardness and love
Is very much unto the Prince and Claudio,
Yet, by mine honour, I will deal in this,
As secretly and justly as your soul   10
Should with your body.

LEONATO: Being that I flow in grief,
The smallest twine may lead me.

FRIAR: 'Tis well consented, presently away,
For to strange sores, strangely they strain the cure,   15
Come Lady, die to live, this wedding day
Perhaps is but prolong'd, have patience and endure.
                Exeunt all but Benedick and Beatrice.

BENEDICK: Lady Beatrice, have you wept all this while?

BEATRICE: Yea, and I will weep a while longer.   20

BENEDICK: I will not desire that.

BEATRICE: You have no reason, I do it freely.

BENEDICK: Surely I do believe your fair cousin is wronged.

BEATRICE: Ah, how much might the man deserve of me
that would right her!   25

BENEDICK: Is there any way to show such friendship?

BEATRICE: A very even way, but no such friend.

BENEDICK: May a man do it?

BEATRICE: It is a man's office, but not yours.

BENEDICK: I do love nothing in the world so well as you,   30
is not that strange?

BEATRICE: As strange as the thing I know not, it were as
possible for me to say, I loved nothing so well as you, but

believe me not, and yet I lie not, I confess nothing, nor I deny nothing, I am sorry for my cousin.

BENEDICK: By my sword Beatrice, thou lovest me.

BEATRICE: Do not swear and eat it.

5 BENEDICK: I will swear by it that you love me, and I will make him eat it that says I love not you.

BEATRICE: Will you not eat your word?

BENEDICK: With no sauce that can be devised to it, I protest I love thee.

10 BEATRICE: Why then God forgive me.

BENEDICK: What offence sweet Beatrice?

BEATRICE: You have stayed me in a happy hour, I was about to protest I loved you.

BENEDICK: And do it with all thy heart.

15 BEATRICE: I love you with so much of my heart, that none is left to protest.

BENEDICK: Come bid me do any thing for thee.

BEATRICE: Kill Claudio.

BENEDICK: Ha, not for the wide world.

20 BEATRICE: You kill me to deny it, farewell.

BENEDICK: Tarry sweet Beatrice.

BEATRICE: I am gone, though I am here, there is no love in you, nay I pray you let me go.

BENEDICK: Beatrice.

25 BEATRICE: In faith I will go.

BENEDICK: We'll be friends first.

BEATRICE: You dare easier be friends with me, than fight with mine enemy.

BENEDICK: Is Claudio thine enemy?

30 BEATRICE: Is a' not approved in the height a villain, that hath slandered, scorned, dishonoured my kinswoman? O that I were a man! what, bear her in hand, until they come to take hands, and then with public accusation

uncovered slander, unmitigated rancour? O God that I
were a man! I would eat his heart in the market place.

BENEDICK: Hear me Beatrice.

BEATRICE: Talk with a man out at a window, a proper
saying. 5

BENEDICK: Nay but Beatrice.

BEATRICE: Sweet Hero, she is wrong'd, she is slander'd,
she is undone.

BENEDICK: Beat –

BEATRICE: Princes and Counties! surely a princely testi- 10
mony, a goodly Count, Count Comfect, a sweet gallant
surely, O that I were a man for his sake! or that I had any
friend would be a man for my sake! But manhood is
mèlted into curtsies, valour into compliment, and men
are only turn'd into tongue, and trim ones too: he is now 15
as valiant as Hercules, that only tells a lie, and swears it: I
cannot be a man with wishing, therefore I will die a
woman with grieving.

BENEDICK: Tarry good Beatrice, by this hand I love thee.

BEATRICE: Use it for my love some other way than swear- 20
ing by it.

BENEDICK: Think you in your soul the Count Claudio
hath wrong'd Hero?

BEATRICE: Yea, as sure as I have a thought, or a soul.

BENEDICK: Enough, I am engag'd, I will challenge him, I 25
will kiss your hand, and so I leave you: by this hand,
Claudio shall render me a dear account: as you hear of
me, so think of me: go comfort your cousin, I must say
she is dead, and so farewell.

Exeunt. 30

IV.2

*Enter Dogberry, Verges, and the Town Clerk, in gowns;
and the Watch, with Conrade and Borachio.*

DOGBERRY: Is our whole dissembly appear'd?

5 VERGES: O a stool and a cushion for the Sexton.

SEXTON: Which be the malefactors?

DOGBERRY: Mary that am I, and my partner.

VERGES: Nay that's certain, we have the exhibition to examine.

10 SEXTON: But which are the offenders that are to be examined? let them come before master constable.

DOGBERRY: Yea mary, let them come before me, what is your name, friend?

BORACHIO: Borachio.

15 DOGBERRY: Pray write down Borachio. Yours sirrah.

CONRADE: I am a gentleman sir, and my name is Conrade.

DOGBERRY: Write down Master Gentleman Conrade: masters, do you serve God?

BOTH: Yea sir we hope.

20 DOGBERRY: Write down, that they hope they serve God: and write God first, for God defend but God should go before such villains: masters, it is proved already that you are little better than false knaves, and it will go near to be thought so shortly, how answer you for your-

25 selves?

CONRADE: Mary sir we say, we are none.

DOGBERRY: A marvellous witty fellow I assure you, but I will go about with him: come you hither sirrah, a word in your ear sir, I say to you, it is thought you are false

30 knaves.

BORACHIO: Sir, I say to you, we are none.

DOGBERRY: Well, stand aside, 'fore God they are both in a tale: have you writ down, that they are none?

SEXTON: Master Constable, you go not the way to examine, you must call forth the watch that are their accusers.   5

DOGBERRY: Yea mary, that's the eftest way, let the watch come forth: masters, I charge you in the Prince's name accuse these men.

WATCH 1: This man said sir, that Don John the Prince's brother was a villain.   10

DOGBERRY: Write down, Prince John a villain: why this is flat perjury, to call a Prince's brother villain.

BORACHIO: Master Constable.

DOGBERRY: Pray thee fellow peace, I do not like thy look I promise thee.   15

SEXTON: What heard you him say else?

WATCH 2: Mary that he had received a thousand ducats of Don John, for accusing the Lady Hero wrongfully.

DOGBERRY: Flat burglary as ever was committed.

VERGES: Yea by mass that it is.   20

SEXTON: What else fellow?

WATCH 1: And that Count Claudio did mean upon his words, to disgrace Hero before the whole assembly, and not marry her.

DOGBERRY: O villain! thou wilt be condemn'd into everlasting redemption for this.   25

SEXTON: What else?

WATCH: This is all.

SEXTON: And this is more masters than you can deny. Prince John is this morning secretly stolen away: Hero   30
was in this manner accus'd, in this very manner refus'd, and upon the grief of this suddenly died: Master Constable, let these men be bound, and brought

to Leonato's, I will go before and show him their
examination.   *Exit.*

DOGBERRY: Come let them be opinion'd.

VERGES: Let them be in the hands –

5 CONRADE: Off, coxcomb!

DOGBERRY: God's my life, where's the Sexton? let him
write down the Prince's officer Coxcomb: come, bind
them, thou naughty varlet.

CONRADE: Away, you are an ass, you are an ass.

10 DOGBERRY: Dost thou not suspect my place? dost thou
not suspect my years? O that he were here to write me
down an ass! but masters, remember that I am an ass,
though it be not written down, yet forget not that I am
an ass: No thou villain, thou art full of piety as shall be

15 prov'd upon thee by good witness, I am a wise fellow,
and which is more, an officer, and which is more, a house-
holder, and which is more, as pretty a piece of flesh as any
is in Messina, and one that knows the Law, go to, and a
rich fellow enough, go to, and a fellow that hath had

20 losses, and one that hath two gowns, and every thing
handsome about him: bring him away: O that I had been
writ down an ass!

Exeunt.

V.I

25   *Enter Leonato and his brother.*

ANTONIO: If you go on thus, you will kill yourself,
      And 'tis not wisdom thus to second grief,
      Against yourself.

LEONATO: I pray thee cease thy counsel,

30   Which falls into mine ears as profitless,
      As water in a sieve: give me not counsel,

Nor let no comforter delight mine ear,
But such a one whose wrongs do suit with mine.
Bring me a father that so lov'd his child,
Whose joy of her is overwhelm'd like mine,
And bid him speak of patience, 5
Measure his woe the length and breadth of mine,
And let it answer every strain for strain,
As thus for thus, and such a grief for such,
In every lineament, branch, shape, and form:
If such a one will smile and stroke his beard, 10
And sorrow, wag, cry hem, when he should groan,
Patch grief with proverbs, make misfortune drunk,
With candle-wasters: bring him yet to me,
And I of him will gather patience:
But there is no such man, for brother, men 15
Can counsel and speak comfort to that grief,
Which they themselves not feel, but tasting it,
Their counsel turns to passion, which before,
Would give preceptial medicine to rage,
Fetter strong madness in a silken thread, 20
Charm ache with air, and agony with words,
No, no, 'tis all men's office, to speak patience
To those that wring under the load of sorrow
But no man's virtue nor sufficiency
To be so moral, when he shall endure 25
The like himself: therefore give me no counsel,
My griefs cry louder than advertisement.
ANTONIO: Therein do men from children nothing differ.
LEONATO: I pray thee peace, I will be flesh and blood,
For there was never yet Philosopher, 30
That could endure the toothache patiently,
However they have writ the style of gods,
And made a push at chance and sufferance.

ANTONIO: Yet bend not all the harm upon yourself,
    Make those that do offend you, suffer too.
LEONATO: There thou speak'st reason, nay I will do so,
    My soul doth tell me, Hero is belied,
5   And that shall Claudio know, so shall the Prince,
    And all of them that thus dishonour her.
                Enter the Prince and Claudio.
ANTONIO: Here comes the Prince and Claudio hastily.
DON PEDRO: Good den, good den.
10 CLAUDIO: Good day to both of you.
LEONATO: Hear you my Lords?
DON PEDRO: We have some haste Leonato.
LEONATO: Some haste my Lord! well, fare you well my
    Lord,
15   Are you so hasty now? well, all is one.
DON PEDRO: Nay do not quarrel with us, good old man.
ANTONIO: If he could right himself with quarrelling,
    Some of us would lie low.
CLAUDIO: Who wrongs him?
20 LEONATO: Marry thou dost wrong me, thou dissembler,
    thou:
    Nay, never lay thy hand upon thy sword,
    I fear thee not.
CLAUDIO: Marry beshrew my hand,
25   If it should give your age such cause of fear,
    In faith my hand meant nothing to my sword.
LEONATO: Tush, tush man, never fleer and jest at me,
    I speak not like a dotard, nor a fool,
    As under privilege of age to brag,
30   What I have done being young, or what would do,
    Were I not old, know Claudio to thy head,
    Thou hast so wrong'd mine innocent child and me,
    That I am forc'd to lay my reverence by,

And, with grey hairs and bruise of many days,
Do challenge thee to trial of a man:
I say thou hast belied mine innocent child.
Thy slander hath gone through and through her heart,
And she lies buried with her ancestors: 5
O in a tomb where never scandal slept,
Save this of hers, fram'd by thy villainy.

CLAUDIO: My villainy?

LEONATO: Thine Claudio, thine I say.

DON PEDRO: You say not right old man.   10

LEONATO: My Lord, my Lord,
I 'll prove it on his body if he dare,
Despite his nice fence, and his active practice,
His May of youth, and bloom of lustihood.

CLAUDIO: Away, I will not have to do with you.   15

LEONATO: Canst thou so daff me? thou hast kill'd my
    child,
If thou kill'st me, boy, thou shalt kill a man.

ANTONIO: He shall kill two of us, and men indeed,
But that 's no matter, let him kill one first: 20
Win me and wear me, let him answer me,
Come follow me boy, come sir boy, come follow me
Sir boy, I 'll whip you from your foining fence,
Nay, as I am a gentleman, I will.

LEONATO: Brother.   25

ANTONIO: Content yourself, God knows, I loved my
    niece,
And she is dead, slander'd to death by villains,
That dare as well answer a man indeed,
As I dare take a serpent by the tongue,   30
Boys, apes, braggarts, Jacks, milksops.

LEONATO: Brother Antony.

ANTONIO: Hold you content, what man! I know them, yea

And what they weigh, even to the utmost scruple,
Scambling, out-facing, fashion-monging boys,
That lie, and cog, and flout, deprave, and slander,
Go antiquely, and show outward hideousness,

5   And speak off half a dozen dang'rous words,
How they might hurt their enemies, if they durst,
And this is all.

LEONATO: But brother Antony.
ANTONIO: Come 'tis no matter,

10   Do not you meddle, let me deal in this.
DON PEDRO: Gentlemen both, we will not wake your
      patience,
My heart is sorry for your daughter's death:
But on my honour she was charg'd with nothing

15   But what was true, and very full of proof.
LEONATO: My Lord, my Lord.
DON PEDRO: I will not hear you.
LEONATO: No: come brother, away, I will be heard.
ANTONIO: And shall, or some of us will smart for it.

20   *Exeunt Leonato and Antonio. Enter Benedick.*
DON PEDRO: See see, here comes the man we went to seek.
CLAUDIO: Now signior, what news?
BENEDICK: Good day my Lord.
DON PEDRO: Welcome signior, you are almost come to

25   part almost a fray.
CLAUDIO: We had like to have had our two noses snapp'd
off with two old men without teeth.
DON PEDRO: Leonato and his brother, what think'st thou?
had we fought, I doubt we should have been too young

30   for them.
BENEDICK: In a false quarrel there is no true valour: I came
to seek you both.
CLAUDIO: We have been up and down to seek thee, for

we are high proof melancholy, and would fain have it
beaten away, wilt thou use thy wit?

BENEDICK: It is in my scabbard, shall I draw it?

DON PEDRO: Dost thou wear thy wit by thy side?

CLAUDIO: Never any did so, though very many have been   5
beside their wit: I will bid thee draw, as we do the
minstrels, draw to pleasure us.

DON PEDRO: As I am an honest man he looks pale, art
thou sick, or angry?

CLAUDIO: What courage man: what though care kill'd a   10
cat, thou hast mettle enough in thee to kill care.

BENEDICK: Sir, I shall meet your wit in the career, and you
charge it against me, I pray you choose another subject.

CLAUDIO: Nay then give him another staff, this last was
broke cross.   15

DON PEDRO: By this light he changes more and more, I
think he be angry indeed.

CLAUDIO: If he be, he knows how to turn his girdle.

BENEDICK: Shall I speak a word in your ear?

CLAUDIO: God bless me from a challenge.   20

BENEDICK: You are a villain, I jest not, I will make it good
how you dare, with what you dare, and when you dare:
do me right, or I will protest your cowardice: you have
kill'd a sweet Lady, and her death shall fall heavy on you,
let me hear from you.   25

CLAUDIO: Well I will meet you, so I may have good cheer.

DON PEDRO: What, a feast, a feast?

CLAUDIO: I' faith I thank him, he hath bid me to a calf's-
head and a capon, the which if I do not carve most curiously, say my knife's naught, shall I not find a woodcock   30
too?

BENEDICK: Sir your wit ambles well, it goes easily.

DON PEDRO: I'll tell thee how Beatrice prais'd thy wit the

other day: I said thou hadst a fine wit, true said she, a
fine little one: no said I, a great wit: right says she, a
great gross one: nay said I, a good wit, just said she, it
hurts nobody: nay said I, the gentleman is wise: certain
5   said she, a wise gentleman: nay said I, he hath the
tongues: that I believe said she, for he swore a thing to
me on Monday night, which he forswore on Tuesday
morning, there's a double tongue, there's two tongues:
thus did she an hour together trans-shape thy particular
10   virtues, yet at last she concluded with a sigh, thou wast
the proper'st man in Italy.

CLAUDIO: For the which she wept heartily and said she
cared not.

DON PEDRO: Yea that she did, but yet for all that, and if
15   she did not hate him deadly, she would love him dearly,
the old man's daughter told us all.

CLAUDIO: All all, and moreover, God saw him when he
was hid in the garden.

DON PEDRO: But when shall we set the savage bull's horns
20   on the sensible Benedick's head?

CLAUDIO: Yea and text underneath, here dwells Benedict
the married man.

BENEDICK: Fare you well, boy, you know my mind, I will
leave you now to your gossip-like humour, you break
25   jests as braggarts do their blades, which God be thanked
hurt not: my Lord, for your many courtesies I thank you,
I must discontinue your company: your brother the
Bastard is fled from Messina: you have among you, kill'd
a sweet and innocent Lady: for my Lord Lack-beard
30   there, he and I shall meet, and till then peace be with
him.

Exit.

DON PEDRO: He is in earnest.

CLAUDIO: In most profound earnest, and I 'll warrant you, for the love of Beatrice.

DON PEDRO: And hath challeng'd thee.

CLAUDIO: Most sincerely.

DON PEDRO: What a pretty thing man is, when he goes in   5
his doublet and hose, and leaves off his wit!

*Enter Dogberry, Verges, and the Watch, with Conrade
and Borachio.*

CLAUDIO: He is then a giant to an ape, but then is an ape
a doctor to such a man.   10

DON PEDRO: But soft you, let me be, pluck up my heart, and be sad, did he not say my brother was fled?

DOGBERRY: Come you sir, if justice cannot tame you, she shall ne'er weigh more reasons in her balance, nay, and you be a cursing hypocrite once, you must be look'd to.   15

DON PEDRO: How now, two of my brother's men bound?
Borachio one.

CLAUDIO: Hearken after their offence my Lord.

DON PEDRO: Officers, what offence have these men done?

DOGBERRY: Mary sir, they have committed false report,   20
moreover they have spoken untruths, secondarily they are slanders, sixth and lastly, they have belied a Lady, thirdly they have verified unjust things, and to conclude, they are lying knaves.

DON PEDRO: First I ask thee what they have done, thirdly   25
I ask thee what 's their offence, sixth and lastly why they are committed, and to conclude, what you lay to their charge.

CLAUDIO: Rightly reasoned, and in his own division, and
by my troth there 's one meaning well suited.   30

DON PEDRO: Who have you offended masters, that you are thus bound to your answer? this learned Constable is too cunning to be understood, what's your offence?

BORACHIO: Sweet Prince, let me go no farther to mine answer: do you hear me, and let this Count kill me: I have deceived even your very eyes: what your wisdoms could not discover, these shallow fools have brought to
5 light, who in the night overheard me confessing to this man, how Don John your brother incensed me to slander the Lady Hero, how you were brought into the orchard, and saw me court Margaret in Hero's garments, how you disgrac'd her when you should marry her: my villainy
10 they have upon record, which I had rather seal with my death, than repeat over to my shame: the lady is dead upon mine and my master's false accusation: and briefly, I desire nothing but the reward of a villain.

DON PEDRO: Runs not this speech like iron through your
15 blood?

CLAUDIO: I have drunk poison whiles he utter'd it.

DON PEDRO: But did my brother set thee on to this?

BORACHIO: Yea, and paid me richly for the practice of it.

20 DON PEDRO: He is compos'd and fram'd of treachery,
And fled he is upon this villainy.

CLAUDIO: Sweet Hero, now thy image doth appear
In the rare semblance that I lov'd it first.

DOGBERRY: Come, bring away the plaintiffs, by this time
25 our sexton hath reformed Signior Leonato of the matter:
and masters, do not forget to specify when time and place shall serve, that I am an ass.

VERGES: Here, here comes Master Signior Leonato, and the sexton too.

30 *Enter Leonato, and Antonio, and the Sexton.*

LEONATO: Which is the villain? let me see his eyes,
That when I note another man like him,
I may avoid him: which of these is he?

BORACHIO: If you would know your wronger, look on
 me.
LEONATO: Art thou the slave that with thy breath hast
 kill'd
 Mine innocent child?   5
BORACHIO: Yea, even I alone.
LEONATO: No, not so villain, thou beliest thyself,
 Here stand a pair of honourable men,
 A third is fled that had a hand in it:
 I thank you Princes for my daughter's death,   10
 Record it with your high and worthy deeds,
 'Twas bravely done, if you bethink you of it.
CLAUDIO: I know not how to pray your patience,
 Yet I must speak, choose your revenge yourself,
 Impose me to what penance your invention   15
 Can lay upon my sin, yet sinn'd I not,
 But in mistaking.
DON PEDRO: By my soul nor I,
 And yet to satisfy this good old man,
 I would bend under any heavy weight,   20
 That he 'll enjoin me to.
LEONATO: I cannot bid you bid my daughter live,
 That were impossible, but I pray you both,
 Possess the people in Messina here,
 How innocent she died, and if your love   25
 Can labour aught in sad invention,
 Hang her an epitaph upon her tomb,
 And sing it to her bones, sing it tonight:
 Tomorrow morning come you to my house,
 And since you could not be my son-in-law,   30
 Be yet my nephew: my brother hath a daughter,
 Almost the copy of my child that 's dead,
 And she alone is heir to both of us,

Give her the right you should have given her cousin,
And so dies my revenge.

CLAUDIO: O noble sir!
Your over kindness doth wring tears from me,
5 I do embrace your offer and dispose
For henceforth of poor Claudio.

LEONATO: Tomorrow then I will expect your coming,
Tonight I take my leave: this naughty man
Shall face to face be brought to Margaret,
10 Who I believe was pack'd in all this wrong,
Hired to it by your brother.

BORACHIO: No by my soul she was not,
Nor knew not what she did when she spoke to me,
But always hath been just and virtuous,
15 In any thing that I do know by her.

DOGBERRY: Moreover sir, which indeed is not under
white and black, this plaintiff here, the offender, did call
me ass, I beseech you let it be remember'd in his punishment, and also the watch heard them talk of one De-
20 formed, they say he wears a key in his ear and a lock
hanging by it, and borrows money in God's name, the
which he hath us'd so long, and never paid, that now
men grow hard-hearted and will lend nothing for God's
sake: pray you examine him upon that point.

25 LEONATO: I thank thee for thy care and honest pains.

DOGBERRY: Your worship speaks like a most thankful and
reverend youth, and I praise God for you.

LEONATO: There's for thy pains.

DOGBERRY: God save the foundation.

30 LEONATO: Go, I discharge thee of thy prisoner, and I thank
thee.

DOGBERRY: I leave an arrant knave with your worship.
which I beseech your worship to correct yourself, for the

example of others: God keep your worship, I wish your
worship well, God restore you to health, I humbly give
you leave to depart and if a merry meeting may be
wish'd, God prohibit it: come neighbour.

Exeunt Dogberry and Verges.   5

LEONATO: Until tomorrow morning, Lords, farewell.

ANTONIO: Farewell my Lords, we look for you tomorrow.

DON PEDRO: We will not fail.

CLAUDIO: Tonight I'll mourn with Hero.

LEONATO: Bring you these fellows on, we'll talk with 10
Margaret, how her acquaintance grew with this lewd
fellow.

Exeunt.

V.2

Enter Benedick and Margaret.   15

BENEDICK: Pray thee sweet Mistress Margaret, deserve
well at my hands, by helping me to the speech of Beatrice.

MARGARET: Will you then write me a sonnet in praise of
my beauty?

BENEDICK: In so high a style Margaret, that no man living 20
shall come over it, for in most comely truth thou deserv-
est it.

MARGARET: To have no man come over me, why shall I
always keep below stairs?

BENEDICK: Thy wit is as quick as the greyhound's mouth, 25
it catches.

MARGARET: And yours, as blunt as the fencer's foils, which
hit, but hurt not.

BENEDICK: A most manly wit Margaret, it will not hurt a
woman: and so I pray thee call Beatrice, I give thee the 30
bucklers.

MARGARET: Give us the swords, we have bucklers of our own.

BENEDICK: If you use them Margaret, you must put in the pikes with a vice, and they are dangerous weapons for maids.

MARGARET: Well, I will call Beatrice to you, who I think hath legs.

Exit Margaret.

BENEDICK: And therefore will come. The God of love that sits above, and knows me, and knows me, how pitiful I deserve. I mean in singing, but in loving, Leander the good swimmer, Troilus the first employer of pandars, and a whole bookful of these quondam carpet-mongers, whose names yet run smoothly in the even road of a blank verse, why they were never so truly turn'd over and over as my poor self in love: marry I cannot show it in rhyme, I have tried, I can find out no rhyme to Lady but baby, an innocent rhyme: for scorn, horn, a hard rhyme: for school, fool, a babbling rhyme: very ominous endings, no, I was not born under a rhyming planet, nor I cannot woo in festival terms.

Enter Beatrice.

Sweet Beatrice wouldst thou come when I call'd thee?

BEATRICE: Yea signior, and depart when you bid me.

BENEDICK: O stay but till then.

BEATRICE: Then, is spoken: fare you well now, and yet ere I go, let me go with that I came, which is, with knowing what hath pass'd between you and Claudio.

BENEDICK: Only foul words, and thereupon I will kiss thee.

BEATRICE: Foul words is but foul wind, and foul wind is but foul breath, and foul breath is noisome, therefore I will depart unkiss'd.

BENEDICK: Thou hast frighted the word out of his right sense, so forcible is thy wit, but I must tell thee plainly, Claudio undergoes my challenge, and either I must shortly hear from him, or I will subscribe him a coward: and I pray thee now tell me, for which of my bad parts 5 didst thou first fall in love with me?

BEATRICE: For them all together, which maintain'd so politic a state of evil, that they will not admit any good part to intermingle with them: but for which of my good parts did you first suffer love for me? 10

BENEDICK: Suffer love! a good epithet, I do suffer love indeed, for I love thee against my will.

BEATRICE: In spite of your heart I think, alas poor heart, if you spite it for my sake, I will spite it for yours, for I will never love that which my friend hates. 15

BENEDICK: Thou and I are too wise to woo peaceably.

BEATRICE: It appears not in this confession, there's not one wise man among twenty that will praise himself.

BENEDICK: An old, an old instance Beatrice, that liv'd in the time of good neighbours, if a man do not erect in this 20 age his own tomb ere he dies, he shall live no longer in monument, than the bell rings, and the widow weeps.

BEATRICE: And how long is that think you?

BENEDICK: Question, why an hour in clamour and a quarter in rheum, therefore is it most expedient for the 25 wise, if Don Worm (his conscience) find no impediment to the contrary, to be the trumpet of his own virtues, as I am to myself so much for praising myself, who I myself will bear witness is praiseworthy, and now tell me, how doth your cousin? 30

BEATRICE: Very ill.

BENEDICK: And how do you?

BEATRICE: Very ill too.

BENEDICK: Serve God, love me, and mend, there will I
    leave you too, for here comes one in haste.

               Enter Ursula.

URSULA: Madam, you must come to your uncle, yonder's
5   old coil at home, it is proved my Lady Hero hath been
    falsely accus'd, the Prince and Claudio mightily abus'd,
    and Don John is the author of all, who is fled and gone:
    will you come presently?

BEATRICE: Will you go hear this news signior?

10 BENEDICK: I will live in thy heart, die in thy lap, and be
    buried in thy eyes: and moreover, I will go with thee to
    thy uncle's.

               Exeunt.

V.3

15   *Enter Don Pedro, Claudio, and three or four with tapers.*

CLAUDIO: Is this the monument of Leonato?

A LORD: It is my Lord.

Epitaph

Done to death by slanderous tongues,
20   *Was the Hero that here lies:*
    Death in guerdon of her wrongs,
    Gives her fame which never dies:
    So the life that died with shame,
    Lives in death with glorious fame.

25   *Hang thou there upon the tomb,*
       Praising her when I am dumb.

CLAUDIO: Now music sound and sing your solemn hymn.

Song

Pardon goddess of the night,
Those that slew thy virgin knight,
For the which with songs of woe,
Round about her tomb they go: 5
Midnight assist our moan, help us to sigh and groan.
Heavily heavily.
Graves yawn and yield your dead,
Till death be uttered,
Heavily heavily.   10

CLAUDIO: Now unto thy bones good night,
  Yearly will I do this rite.
DON PEDRO: Good morrow masters, put your torches out,
  The wolves have prey'd, and look, the gentle day
  Before the wheels of Phoebus, round about   15
  Dapples the drowsy East with spots of grey:
  Thanks to you all, and leave us, fare you well.
CLAUDIO: Good morrow masters, each his several way.
DON PEDRO: Come let us hence, and put on other weeds,
  And then to Leonato's we will go.   20
CLAUDIO: And Hymen now with luckier issue speeds,
  Than this for whom we render'd up this woe.
                    Exeunt.

V.4

Enter Leonato, Benedick, Beatrice, Margaret, Ursula,   25
        Antonio, Friar, and Hero.
FRIAR: Did I not tell you she was innocent?
LEONATO: So are the Prince and Claudio who accus'd her,
  Upon the error that you heard debated:
  But Margaret was in some fault for this,   30

Although against her will as it appears,
In the true course of all the question.

ANTONIO: Well, I am glad that all things sorts so well.

BENEDICK: And so am I, being else by faith enforc'd
5   To call young Claudio to a reckoning for it.

LEONATO: Well daughter, and you gentlewomen all,
Withdraw into a chamber by yourselves,
And when I send for you come hither masked:
The Prince and Claudio promis'd by this hour
10   To visit me: you know your office brother,
You must be father to your brother's daughter,
And give her to young Claudio.

Exeunt Ladies.

ANTONIO: Which I will do with confirm'd countenance.

15   BENEDICK: Friar, I must entreat your pains, I think.

FRIAR: To do what Signior?

BENEDICK: To bind me, or undo me, one of them:
Signior Leonato, truth it is good Signior,
Your niece regards me with an eye of favour.

20   LEONATO: That eye my daughter lent her, 'tis most true.

BENEDICK: And I do with an eye of love requite her.

LEONATO: That sight whereof I think you had from me,
From Claudio and the Prince, but what's your will?

BENEDICK: Your answer sir is enigmatical,
25   But for my will, my will is, your good will
May stand with ours, this day to be conjoin'd,
In the state of honourable marriage,
In which (good Friar) I shall desire your help.

LEONATO: My heart is with your liking.

30   FRIAR: And my help.
Here comes the Prince and Claudio.

Enter Don Pedro, and Claudio, and two or three others.

DON PEDRO: Good morrow to this fair assembly.

LEONATO: Good morrow Prince, good morrow Claudio:
　We here attend you: are you yet determined,
　Today to marry with my brother's daughter?
CLAUDIO: I'll hold my mind were she an Ethiope.
LEONATO: Call her forth brother, here's the Friar ready. 　5
Exit Antonio.
DON PEDRO: Good morrow Benedick, why what's the
　matter?
　That you have such a February face,
　So full of frost, of storm, and cloudiness. 　10
CLAUDIO: I think he thinks upon the savage bull:
　Tush fear not man, we'll tip thy horns with gold,
　And all Europa shall rejoice at thee,
　As once Europa did at lusty Jove,
　When he would play the noble beast in love. 　15
BENEDICK: Bull Jove sir had an amiable low.
　And some such strange bull leap'd your father's cow,
　And got a calf in that same noble feat,
　Much like to you, for you have just his bleat.
Enter Antonio, with Hero, Beatrice, Margaret, 　20
Ursula, masked.
CLAUDIO: For this I owe you: here comes other reck'n-
　ings.
　Which is the Lady I must seize upon?
ANTONIO: This same is she, and I do give you her. 　25
CLAUDIO: Why then she's mine: sweet, let me see your
　face.
LEONATO: No that you shall not till you take her hand,
　Before this Friar, and swear to marry her.
CLAUDIO: Give me your hand before this holy Friar, 　30
　I am your husband if you like of me.
HERO: And when I liv'd I was your other wife, ⟨*Unmasks*⟩
　And when you loved, you were my other husband.

CLAUDIO: Another Hero.

HERO: Nothing certainer:
    One Hero died defil'd, but I do live,
    And surely as I live, I am a maid.

5 DON PEDRO: The former Hero, Hero that is dead.

LEONATO: She died my Lord, but whiles her slander liv'd.

FRIAR: All this amazement can I qualify,
    When after that the holy rites are ended,
    I'll tell you largely of fair Hero's death:
10   Meantime let wonder seem familiar,
    And to the chapel let us presently.

BENEDICK: Soft and fair Friar, which is Beatrice?

BEATRICE: I answer to that name, what is your will?
                                                ⟨*Unmasks*⟩.

15 BENEDICK: Do not you love me?

BEATRICE: Why no, no more than reason.

BENEDICK: Why then your uncle, and the Prince, and
    Claudio
    Have been deceived, they swore you did.

20 BEATRICE: Do not you love me?

BENEDICK: Troth no, no more than reason.

BEATRICE: Why then my cousin, Margaret and Ursula
    Are much deceiv'd, for they did swear you did.

BENEDICK: They swore that you were almost sick for me.

25 BEATRICE: They swore that you were wellnigh dead for
    me.

BENEDICK: 'Tis no such matter, then you do not love me.

BEATRICE: No truly, but in friendly recompence.

LEONATO: Come cousin, I am sure you love the gentle-
30   man.

CLAUDIO: And I'll be sworn upon 't, that he loves her,
    For here 's a paper written in his hand,
    A halting sonnet of his own pure brain,

Fashioned to Beatrice.

HERO: And here 's another,
Writ in my cousin's hand, stol'n from her pocket,
Containing her affection unto Benedick.

BENEDICK: A miracle, here 's our own hands against our 5
hearts: come, I will have thee, but by this light I take
thee for pity.

BEATRICE: I would not deny you, but by this good day, I
yield upon great persuasion, and partly to save your life,
for I was told, you were in a consumption. 10

BENEDICK: Peace I will stop your mouth.

DON PEDRO: How dost thou Benedick the married man?

BENEDICK: I 'll tell thee what Prince: a college of wit-
crackers cannot flout me out of my humour, dost thou
think I care for a satire or an epigram? no, if a man will 15
be beaten with brains, a' shall wear nothing handsome
about him: in brief, since I do purpose to marry, I will
think nothing to any purpose that the world can say
against it, and therefore never flout at me, for what I have
said against it: for man is a giddy thing, and this is my 20
conclusion: for thy part Claudio, I did think to have
beaten thee, but in that thou art like to be my kinsman,
live unbruis'd, and love my cousin.

CLAUDIO: I had well hop'd thou wouldst have denied
Beatrice, that I might have cudgell'd thee out of thy 25
single life, to make thee a double dealer, which out of
question thou wilt be, if my cousin do not look exceeding
narrowly to thee.

BENEDICK: Come, come, we are friends, let 's have a
dance ere we are married, that we may lighten our own 30
hearts, and our wives' heels.

LEONATO: We 'll have dancing afterward.

BENEDICK: First, of my word, therefore play music::

Prince, thou art sad, get thee a wife, get thee a wife, there
is no staff more reverend than one tipp'd with horn.

Enter Messenger.

MESSENGER: My Lord, your brother John is ta'en in flight,
5   And brought with armed men back to Messina.

BENEDICK: Think not on him till tomorrow, I 'll devise
three brave punishments for him: strike up pipers.

Dance.

Exeunt.

NOTES

References are to the page and line of this edition;
there are 33 lines to the full page.

Stage Direction: Innogen his wife: This lady, who re- P. 23 L. 2
appears at the beginning of Act II, takes no part in the
play. See Introduction, p. 18. The general situation at
the beginning of the play, with the gallants returning
from a campaign which brought much glory and
little loss, is similar to the events of August of 1596
when the many gallants who had gone to Cadiz returned to London.

Don Pedro: the old texts here call him Peter.   P. 23 L. 16

badge: the master's coat-of-arms in metal worn on a P. 23 L. 24
servant's sleeve. It still survives in 'Doggett's coat and
badge', the prize annually given to the winner of the
Thames watermen's race. *Badge of bitterness:* sign that
it is servant to bitterness.

Signior Mountanto: 'Master Thruster'. *Mountanto:* a P. 24 L. 1
thrust in fencing.

He set . . . burbolt: The point of Beatrice's jest is vari- P. 24 LL. 9–
ously explained by editors (i.e., no one understands   12
it). *Set up his bills:* put up a poster; *at the flight:* at a
shooting match; *subscrib'd:* signed for; *burbolt:* bird-
bolt, a short blunt arrow for killing birds.

be meet with you: be even with you.   P. 24 L. 16

five wits: i.e., common sense, imagination, fantasy, P. 25 L. 1
estimation, memory.

jade's trick: spiteful trick, a *jade* being a vicious horse. P. 27 L. 12

bid you welcome . . . duty: Spoken to Don John. It is P. 27 LL.
easy to overlook this morose and malevolent gentle-   21–2
man in the reading; on the stage he is more conspicu-
ous.

play . . . carpenter: 'or are you mocking us by pre- P. 28 LL.
tending that contraries are truths, as that *blind* Cupid 14–16

can catch hares or that *blacksmith* Vulcan is a carpenter'. *Flouting Jack*: mocking knave.

P. 28 L. 33 *Enter Don Pedro*: the Quarto reads *Enter don Pedro, John the bastard*, but this seems an obvious error.

P. 29 L. 4 *charge thee on thy allegiance*: the most solemn of all commands, for to disobey is high treason. Benedick so commanded cannot choose but betray Claudio's secret.

P. 29 LL. 11– *Like the old tale ... should be so*: There are various
12 versions, one of which runs thus. A Lady unexpectedly went to visit the house of Mr Fox. Finding no one at home she entered and came to a door inscribed *Be bold*. She went further and found another door inscribed *Be bold, be bold*: further still, another door inscribed *Be bold, be bold, be not too bold*. At this she spied Mr Fox coming into the house, dragging a young woman by the hair. The Lady hid herself. Mr Fox tried in vain to wrench a ring from the young woman's hand, and then with his sword impatiently chopped off the hand, which flew into the air and fell by the Lady. She took the hand and escaped unseen. Soon afterwards Mr Fox came to her house to dinner. The Lady began to tell the tale of her adventure to the guests, as if it had been a dream. At every pause Mr Fox observed, 'It is not so, nor 'twas not so: but indeed, God forbid it should be so.' At length the Lady reached the climax of the tale, with 'But it was so, and it is so; and here's the hand I have to show'. Whereupon the others fell upon Mr Fox and slew him.

P. 29 L. 17 *fetch me in*: make me commit myself.

P. 30 L. 1 *recheat*: a call on the horn to summon the hounds. Benedick is playing on the inevitable joke that married men whose wives are faithless are said to wear invisible horns.

P. 30 L. 11 *ballad-maker's pen*: Any sensational event, especially the tragic death of a criminal or forlorn lover, was at once celebrated by a ballad.

P. 30 L. 12 *blind Cupid*: The usual sign set outside a brothel.

in a bottle like a cat: A cat, enclosed in a wicker basket, P. 30 L. 16
was sometimes the target for archers.

Adam: possibly Adam Bell, a famous archer. If so P. 30 L. 18
call'd Adam: hailed as a crack shot.

in time the savage bull doth bear the yoke: a famous line P. 30 LL.
in Kyd's *The Spanish Tragedy* (c. 1586), the most 19–20
popular and most parodied of all Elizabethan plays.

Cupid ... Venice: Venice was noted for the number P. 30 LL.
and the magnificence of its courtesans. 29–30

temporize with the hours: in time you will come to P. 30 L. 32
terms.

so I leave you: This passage of prose dialogue is a good P. 31 LL.
specimen of the witty conversation of gallants of 12–13
Shakespeare's time. The dialogue passes abruptly into
a rather stiff verse, which may be a relic of an earlier
version of the play but certainly changes the mood
from light banter to serious conversation.

And I will break with her: Marriages amongst those of P. 32 L. 3
good family were carefully arranged and the negotia-
tions often conducted by third parties. Claudio thus
shows normal prudence. First he asks after Hero's
prospects, and then obtains the best possible agent to
negotiate for him.

The Prince and Count Claudio: The misunderstandings P. 33 LL. 2–3
of this episode are complex and never wholly cleared
up.

thick pleached alley: a path sheltered by a thick hedge P. 33 L. 3
with interlaced boughs – a common feature in old
formal gardens.

by the top: by the forelock. P. 33 L. 8

What the goodyear: a phrase whose origin is not yet P. 33 l. 23
satisfactorily explained, meaning much as 'what the
hell'.

born under Saturn: therefore melancholy and grim. P. 34 L. 1

fashion ... love: to force my manners to be ingratiat- P. 34 L. 17
ing.

smoking: burning perfume in. P. 35 L. 11

P. 36 L. 2   *heart-burn'd:* suffer indigestion from too much acidity.

P. 36 L. 25   *in the woollen:* in blankets without sheets – tickling to the skin.

P. 36 L. 33   *Berrord:* bear-ward, the keeper of the bears for baiting.

P. 36 L. 33   *apes into hell:* this was supposed to be the fate of those who died maids.

P. 37 L. 30   *Scotch jig:* a lively dance.

P. 37 L. 30   *measure:* a grave formal dance.

P. 37 L. 30   *cinque pace:* the first five steps of a galliard, 'a swift and wandering dance . . . with passages uncertain to and fro', as Sir John Davies called it in *Orchestra*, a poem of dancing.

P. 38 L. 8   *Enter Don Pedro . . . :* The stage direction both in Quarto and Folio reads '*or dumbe John*'. There is a similar visit of masquers in *Romeo and Juliet* (I. 4–5). The gentlemen, masked, go up to the ladies who are unmasked, and take partners. As they dance each couple pass in front of the stage, speak their lines, and give way to the next couple – a procedure which requires skilled producing and accurate timing.

P. 38 L. 10   *walk about:* i.e., be my partner in the measure.

P. 38 L. 17   *God defend:* God forbid.

P. 38 L. 19   *Philemon's roof:* Baucis and Philemon, a poor and ancient couple, entertained the gods Jupiter and Mercury unawares in their thatched cottage.

P. 39 L. 19   *Hundred Merry Tales:* a famous jest book, first printed in 1526.

P. 39 L. 31   *in the Fleet:* in the company sailing round.

P. 40 L. 26   *to the banquet:* to the refreshments.

P. 41 L. 11   *next willow:* because the willow garland is the sign of a deserted lover.

P. 41 L. 31   *world into her person:* claims to know what the world thinks.

P. 42 LL. 4–5 *lodge in a warren:* game-keeper's cottage – a solitary spot.

Hercules . . . spit: to turn the spits on which the meat P. 43 LL. 6–7
was roasted was one of the tasks of the 'black guard',
the lowest menials.

Ate: goddess of strife. P. 43 L. 9

scholar would conjure her: Latin was the proper P. 43 LL. 9–
language in which to control spirits: a scholar was 10
therefore necessary.

tooth-picker: Tooth-picks were still regarded as P. 43 L. 20
foreign and rather fantastic articles.

Prester John: A mythical King, vastly rich, of Abys- P. 43 L. 21
sinia or the unknown parts beyond.

great Cham: the Emperor of the Mongols. Benedick P. 43 L. 22
will undertake a journey to the farthest and most
dangerous kingdoms to avoid Beatrice' tongue.

civil as an orange: with a pun on Seville whence the P. 44 L. 14
oranges came. *Jealous complexion:* yellow – the colour
of jealousy.

Good Lord for alliance: 'Good Lord, what a thing this P. 45 L. 4
marrying is.'

sun-burnt: i.e., no beauty, for the fashionable lady of P. 45 L. 5
the time was careful to keep an ivory complexion by
avoiding sun-tan.

Margaret term me Claudio: Critics have been much P. 48 L. 14
troubled by this detail, for, they reasonably argue,
Margaret must have suspected something, yet later is
exonerated from all blame. The best suggestion is by
Miss Grace Trenery in the Arden Shakespeare: 'Borachio evidently means to persuade Margaret to dress
up in Hero's clothes and, thus disguised as her mistress, to act with him a love-scene in which the servants shall pretend to be their "betters", a game well
calculated to appeal to the mad-cap Margaret.
Claudio is to be placed where he can witness this
encounter between his betrothed and another man,
and his sense of outrage will naturally be increased by
the fact that they are making mock of his honourable
suit.'

tabor and the pipe: the traditional music of shepherds, P. 49 LL.
clowns, and other men of peace. *Tabor:* a small drum. 17–18

P. 49 L. 20   *doublet:* coat, often elaborately cut and embroidered.

P. 49 LL. 22–3 *turn'd orthography:* become a maker of fine phrases.

P. 50 L. 3   *noble ... angel:* a common pun, both words being also the names of coins, the 'noble' being worth 6s 8d, the 'angel' 10s.

P. 50 L. 13   *We'll ... pennyworth:* 'we'll give the clever fool something for his money'. Editors usually alter to *hid fox.* The reference is however to the story of the Kid and the Fox (told for instance in Spenser's *Shepherd's Calendar* – May), the Kid, for all his conceit, being deceived and carried off by the Fox.

       Such end had the Kid, for he nould warnéd be
       Of craft, coloured with simplicity.

P. 51 L. 2   *horn ... money:* Benedick is no lover of chamber music.

P. 51 L. 21   *for a shift:* to serve the turn.

P. 52 L. 12   *infinite of thought:* beyond even the infinite limits of imagination.

P. 53 L. 15   *half-pence:* small fragments. Pennies were still made of silver, about the size of the modern sixpence but thinner.

P. 55 L. 18   *dumb-show:* a device often used in tragic drama. Before the play, and sometimes before each act, the characters silently mimed the action which was to follow. There is a dumb-show before the play scene in *Hamlet,* III. 2.

P. 55 LL. 23–4 *full bent:* are tightly stretched, like a strung bow.

P. 56 L. 5   *sentences:* proverbs, wise sayings, such as the 'few sentences' which Polonius bestowed on Laertes. (*Hamlet,* I. 3.)

P. 57 LL. 11–12 *like favourites ... bred it:* This striking simile would inevitably have reminded the original spectators of the Earl of Essex, who from his quarrel with Queen Elizabeth in June 1598 until his death in February 1601 continually 'advanced his pride' against the Queen.

P. 57 L. 14   *propose:* conversation. The Folio alters to 'purpose'.

lapwing: the lapwing, like the partridge, runs swiftly P. 57 L. 27
along the ground.

golden oars: Shakespeare is thinking of roach or perch P. 57 L. 31
fishing in clear water; red and golden are often taken
as the same colour in Shakespeare.

wood-bine coverture: the hiding-place grown over with P. 58 L. 3
honeysuckle.

haggerds: A haggerd is a young wild hawk, as yet P. 58 L. 9
untamed.

wrastle with affection: overcome his love. P. 58 L. 16

spell him backward: 'turn him inside out.' P. 59 L. 3

agate: the device cut in a seal ring. P. 59 L. 7

press me to death: The punishment of pressing to P. 59 L. 18
death was inflicted on those who refused to plead at
trial. Weights were piled on the accused until he died.

What fire ... : This sudden change into rhymed P. 60 L. 18
verse may be a relic of an earlier version of the play,
but aesthetically it is right and revealing. Beatrice for
all her light chatter can be moved to deep emotion
(which is properly expressed in verse) as well as the
others.

hang it first, and draw it afterwards: The tooth-drawer P. 61 L. 25
used to display his trophies on a string; but hanging
and drawing inevitably suggests the punishment of a
traitor who was first hanged, then cut down while
still alive; after which his entrails were drawn out
and burnt, and the body hacked into quarters.

humour or a worm: humour has a variety of meanings: P. 61 L. 27
in this context it means either a damp rottenness or a
cold. *A worm*: rotten teeth were supposed to be
caused by small worms.

a Dutchman today ... doublet: It was a common joke P. 62 LL. 2–5
that the Englishman borrowed his fashions from
every country in Europe.

tennis balls: at this time made of leather stuffed with P. 62 L. 14
hair.

civet: perfume made from glandular secretions of the P. 62 L. 17
civet cat.

P. 62 L. 21   *his melancholy:* The true lover revealed his state by
              acute melancholy, and (as Rosalind expressed it)
              everything about him 'demonstrating a careless deso-
              lation'.

P. 62 L. 22   *wash his face:* i.e., with perfume.

P. 62 L. 33   *dies for him:* dies for love of him.

P. 63 L. 1   *her face upwards:* Editors fuss over this phrase, which
              is but another version of the broad jests of Margaret
              (p. 71, l. 8).

P. 63 L. 4   *hobby-horses:* The hobby-horse is an imitation horse
              worn by a morris dancer, who prances and leaps
              about with it: so *hobby-horse:* buffoon.

P. 65 L. 2   *the Watch:* In Shakespeare's time there was no regu-
              lar police force. Each parish appointed a constable.
              When a watch was needed sober and substantial
              citizens were called upon to do their duty. Clashes
              between the Watch and young gallants were com-
              mon. Thus on 6th July, 1600

                   'in the Star Chamber Sir Edward Baynham and
              three gentlemen for riots and misdemeanours were
              fined £200 each and imprisonment. They had gone
              to supper in Bread Street at the "Mermaid", and there
              they supped and there they stayed until 2 o'clock in
              disorder and excess of drink; and then they departed
              with rapiers drawn, and menaced, wounded and beat
              the watch in Friday Street and Paul's Churchyard,
              uttering seditious words. The Lord Chief Justice, the
              Lord Treasurer and the Lord Keeper were for fining
              Williamson, the taverner, £40, but because he was
              known an honest man and of good government, and
              would not suffer music or illegal games in house, and
              sent for the Constable to keep good order, he was
              acquitted'. [*3rd Elizabethan Journal,* p. 97.] Thomas
              Dekker in Chapter VIII of *The Gull's Hornbook* gives
              mock advice to the gallant on night walking, 'and
              how to pass by any watch'. 'If you smell a watch,
              and that you may easily do, for commonly they eat
              onions to keep them in sleeping, which they account
              a medicine against cold; or, if you come within

danger of their brown bills; let him that is your
candlestick, and holds up your torch from dropping,
for to march after a link is shoemaker-like; let *ignis
fatuus*, I say, being within the reach of the constable's
staff, ask aloud, "Sir Giles" – or "Sir Abram" – "will
you turn this way, or down that street?" It skills not,
though there be none dubbed in your bunch; the
watch will wink at you, only for the love they bear
to arms and knighthood. Marry, if the sentinel and
his court of guard stand strictly upon his martial law,
and cry "Stand", commanding you to give the word,
and to shew reason why your ghost walks so late; do
it in some jest: for that will show you have a desperate wit, and perhaps make him and his halberdiers
afraid to lay foul hands upon you; or, if you read a
mittimus in the constable's book; counterfeit to be a
Frenchman, a Dutchman, or any other nation whose
country is in peace with your own, and you may pass
the pikes; for, being not able to understand you, they
cannot by the customs of the city take your examination, and so by consequence they have nothing to say
to you'. [Edited by R. B. McKerrow, pp. 77–8.]

salvation: i.e., damnation. Shakespeare's lowly born P. 65 L. 5
characters often love to use long words with many
meanings.

to be well-favoured: Dogberry as usual gets it wrong. P. 65 L. 16
To be handsome (well-favoured) is the gift of
Nature; Fortune brings other attainments, such as
learning. Celia and Rosalind argue the matter with
greater discretion. (*As You Like it*, I. ii.)

vagrom: vagabonds, always much suspected by P. 65 L. 26
Authority.

bills: the watchman's weapon; it was adapted from P. 66 L. 11
the hedger's tool, mounted on a longer shaft.

Enter Borachio and Conrade: It is usually Shakespeare's P. 67 L. 30
custom in a story of intrigue and misunderstanding
to show the audience what is happening. In this way
he gains the greater emotional effect of dramatic
irony, for when we know the truth we can appreciate
significances in the dialogue unsuspected by the

speakers. Hero's troubles are more poignant when
they can be seen approaching. The name Borachio
means drunkard.

P. 68 L. 27   *I know that deformed . . . :* There is a topical allusion
here, now lost. Ben Jonson also in *Cynthia's Revels*
apparently satirizes the same person in the character
of 'Amorphus, or the deformed: one that hath drunk
of the fountain [of self-love]'.

P. 70 L. 2   *wears a lock:* i.e., a love lock.

P. 70 LL. 8–9   *commodity . . . bills:* literally a parcel of merchandize
obtained on credit against an acknowledgement of
the debt – with a pun on the watchmen's 'bills'.

P. 70 L. 20   *rebato . . . :* The various articles of Hero's clothing are
thus defined by Miss M. C. Linthicum in *Costume in
Elizabethan Drama: rebato:* 'After 1570, ladies' closed
ruffs gave place to those open in front and set up fan-
wise from the low-cut neck-line. . . . This style was
worn especially by unmarried women. The open ruff
was supported by a linen-covered, wire frame, called
rebato.' *Down sleeves, side sleeves:* 'Margaret's description of the Duchess of Milan's gown as having
"down sleeves, side sleeves" is not as difficult of ex-
planation as some editors think. The down sleeves
were long sleeves to the wrist; the side sleeve, the
hanging or pendant sleeve, open from the shoulder.'
Cuts: Italian cutwork. 'It was made by cutting away
the material in squares, and filling the spaces with
geometric designs of needlework'. *Round underborne:* 'worn over bluish tinsel'. *Tire:* manner of
dressing the hair. *Night-gown:* 'A night-gown was
an ankle-length gown with long sleeves and collar
varying in size from the shawl-collar of the men's
modern dressing-gown to the fur collar on ladies'
coats.'

P. 71 L. 13   *saving your reverence:* the phrase, often abbreviated to
'sirreverence', is an apology for an improper word.

P. 71 L. 24   *Light a' love:* a popular dance tune.

P. 71 L. 25   *burden:* undersong, sung by the male bass voice.

P. 71 L. 28   *barns:* with a pun on 'bairns'.

five a' clock: Elizabethan weddings took all day. They P. 71 L. 31
began early with the fetching of the bride to church
by the bridegroom and his friends, and ended late
with the noisy putting to bed of bride and bridegroom.

H: H and 'ache' were pronounced alike. P. 72 L. 1

carduus benedictus: 'blessed thistle'. A concoction of P. 72 L. 18
the plant was regarded as a potent medicine for a host
of complaints.

false gallop: canter. P. 73 L. 4

palabras: for *pocas palabras*, few words. P. 73 L. 28

noncome: for non plus, i.e., confusion. P. 75 L. 8

Dian: the chaste Goddess of Hunting, and also in her P. 77 L. 7
heavenly form, the Moon.

wide: i.e., so far from the truth. P. 77 L. 12

on the rearward of: i.e., following close after. P. 79 L. 19

Hear me a little ... mark'd: Both Folio and Quarto P. 80 LL.
print these lines as prose. 15–17

observations ... book: my observation and experience P. 80 LL.
of humanity which confirms (sets the seal on) what 24–6
I have read.

Your ... dead: This is the reading of Quarto and P. 81 L. 30
Folio. Editors usually emend to 'Your daughter
have the Princes left for dead'.

mourning ostentation: outward show of mourning. P. 81 L. 33
Funerals in good families were organized by the
Heralds and celebrated with much pomp.

study of imagination: contemplation. P. 82 L. 20

bear her in hand: lead her on by false promises. P. 84 L. 32

Count Comfect: 'Count Candy'. P. 85 L. 11

IV. 2. The original stage direction is *Enter the Con-* P. 86 L. 1
stables, Borachio, and the Town clearke in gownes; the
Town clerk who in the speech headings becomes
'Sexton'. In the scene the speech headings in the
Qurato instead of *Dogberry* and *Verges* read *Kemp*
and *Cowley*. William Kemp was the Clown of the
Lord Chamberlain's Company, famous for his low
comedy parts. He left the Company in 1599.

P. 86 L. 5   *O a stool and a cushion :* In Verges' eyes the Sexton (who can write) is a great man and must be honoured accordingly.

P. 86 L. 8   *exhibition :* Dogberry, knowing that *inhibition* means 'permission refused' assumes that 'permission granted' should be *exhibition.*

P. 87 L. 6   *eftest :* quickest, a word apparently of Dogberry's invention.

P. 88 LL. 4–5   *Let them be ... coxcomb :* The Quarto reads 'Couley Let them be in the hands of Coxcombe'.

P. 89 L. 11   *And sorrow ... groan :* This is the most disputed line in the play, variously emended and repunctuated. Our text follows the Quarto exactly and may be right. Leonato is so overcome by his passion that thoughts come too quick for grammar to keep up. In modern punctuation the incoherence would be shown thus:
'If such a one will smile and stroke his beard ... And sorrow ... wag, cry "hem" ... Make misfortune drunk with candle-wasters. ...'
The cry 'hem' is a toper's exclamation like 'cheerio'. The line thus means : 'If such a man can be cheery in his sorrow, bring him to me'. The common emendation is 'Bid Sorrow wag, cry "hem!";' i.e., tell Sorrow to wag his beard in gay chatter.

P. 89 L. 13   *candle-wasters :* those who stay up late at night.

P. 89 L. 19   *preceptial medicine :* healing advice.

P. 89 L. 33   *made a push :* made a brave show against.

P. 90 L. 31   *to thy head :* to thy face.

P. 91 L. 14   *May of youth :* Youth in full bloom.

P. 91 L. 18   *boy :* To call a man a boy is to give him a gross insult. Thus Aufidius tempts Coriolanus to lose his temper and his life (*Coriolanus* V. 5).

P. 91 L. 23   *foining fence :* thrusting fence. Antonio as an old man has no use for the new fashioned thrusting rapier affected by such young gallants as Claudio : to him the man's weapon is the old cutting longsword.

P. 92 L. 4   *Go antiquely :* wear fantastic fashions.

draw : with a pun on drawing the fiddler's bow.   P. 93 L. 7

staff . . . broke cross: In tilting the skilled combatant P. 93 LL. broke his tilting spear (staff) full on his opponent's   14–15 shield; the novice who flinched from the impact broke his spear across it.

to turn his girdle: a proverbial saying, used as a retort P. 93 L. 18 to an angry man.

God bless me from: preserve me from.   P. 93 L. 20

You . . . villain: This is a direct insult, and thus a P. 93 L. 21 challenge to a duel.

carve most curiously: expert carving was part of a P. 93 LL. gentleman's education. *Curiously:* artistically.   29–30

an ape a doctor: an ape is a learned man compared P. 95 LL. with.   9–10

in his own division: by his own method of arrange- P. 95 L. 29 ment.

invention: literary composition, i.e., funeral poem.   P. 97 L. 26

Tomorrow . . . nephew: To modern notions it is sur- P. 97. LL. prising that Leonato should still want Claudio for a   29–31 son-in-law; but, as the Prince's favourite, he is a good prize, and practical rather than romantic considera- tions ruled in most marriages.

foundation: i.e., this noble house.   P. 98 L. 29

give . . . bucklers: acknowledge myself beaten.   P. 99 LL. 30–1

pikes with a vice: The buckler was a small shield used P. 100 L. 4 as defence against the longsword. It was sometimes fitted with a spike for thrusting in the opponent's face. *vice:* screw.

so politic a state of evil: so united a state.   P. 101 LL. 7–8

if a man do not erect . . . his own tomb ere he dies: Most P. 101 LL. of the sumptuous Tudor tombs which still survive   20–1 were erected by the occupants – and not by their heirs.

old coil: a slang phrase – 'a rare old fuss!'   P. 102 L. 5

confirm'd countenance: straight face.   P. 104 L. 14

Europa: one of Jupiter's loves whom he courted dis- P. 105 L. 14 guised as a bull.

GLOSSARY

a' : he
affect : love
antique : grotesque
apprehension : quick wit
approved : proved
aspicious : for suspicious
assurance : proof

baldrick : shoulder belt for carrying a horn
basted : sewn together
bate : abate
bent : natural inclination
beshrew : ill luck to
birlady : by Our Lady
blazon : description
block : mould on which a hat is
   made; so new fashion
blood : passion
breathing : breathing space

canker : wild rose
career : charge
carpet-mongers : drawing-room
   knights
claw : stroke
codpiece : opening in the hose
   (breeches)
cog : cheat
coil : confusion, fuss
come over : surpass
complexion : bodily appearance
conjecture : suspicion
contemptible : contemptuous
County : Count
cross : thwart

crossness : perversity
curst : shrewish, bad-tempered

daff'd, daft : thrust aside
daw : jackdaw
defend : forbid
deprave : defame
desartless : for deserving
despite : spite
despite of : despising

earnest : money on account
ecstasy : passion
enfranchis'd : allowed liberty
engag'd : pledged
enrag'd : frantic
even : straight

fain : gladly
fancy : love
fathers : resembles her father
favour : face
fine : end
fleer : flout
frame : framing, invention

good den : good afternoon
guarded : (1) ornamented with
   braid or bars of velvet; (2)
   protected
guerdon : token, reward
gull : trick

haggerds : wild hawks
halting : limping

high-proof: fully tested, in the highest degree

holp: helped

horn-mad: raving mad (with jealousy)

humour: whim

Hymen: god of wedding

important: importunate

invention: intellect, inspiration

inwardness: intimacy

kindness: natural affection

lief as: as soon

luxurious: lustful

marl: clay

misprising: condemning

misprision: misunderstanding

model: plan

moral: (noun) hidden meaning

moral: (adjective) full of moralizings

name: high rank

noncome: for nonplus

noted: made notes on

old ends: odd sayings

once: in a word

opinioned: for pinioned

pack'd: one of the pack, accomplice

penthouse: roof over an open shed

Phoebus: the sun god

pleach'd: see note on *thickpleached* (p. 33, l. 3)

possess: inform

practice: plot

present: (verb) represent

presently: immediately

proposing: conversing

qualify: moderate

quips: jests

quirks: witty sayings

quit me: requite me

quondam: sometimes, former

rack: stretch out

reclusive: shut up

reechy: grimy

rheum: moisture, tears

sad: serious

salv'd: soothed

scambling: shoving

second: support

seven-night: week

slops: baggy breeches

smock: night-gown

sort: rank

sort: turn out

squarer: quarreler

stale: prostitute

still: always

stomach: appetite

stuff'd: have a cold in the nose

subscribe: sign a declaration

sufferance: endurance

suffigance: for sufficient

suit: match

tartly: sourly

tax: criticize, charge

tender: offer

terminations: expressions

throughly : thoroughly
'tis once : once for all, in short
trace : traverse
troth : truth

unconfirm'd : inexperienced
undergoes : endures, receives
utter'd : overcome

us'd : made a habit of

vigitant : for vigilant
visor : mask

wake : disturb
windy : windward
wrastle : wrestle
wring : suffer torment

PENGUIN POPULAR CLASSICS

Published or forthcoming

PENGUIN POPULAR CLASSICS

Published or forthcoming

PENGUIN POPULAR CLASSICS

Published or forthcoming